T0167125

DOGS IN THE CITY

FROM SCRAPS TO STEAKS

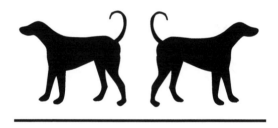

by

A v r i l   P a t t e r s o n - F e c k e r

iUniverse, Inc.
Bloomington

DOGS IN THE CITY
FROM SCRAPS TO STEAKS

Copyright © 2013 Avril Patterson-Fecker, avrilfecker@gmail.com

All rights reserved. No part of this book may be used or reproduced by any means, graphic, electronic, or mechanical, including photocopying, recording, taping or by any information storage retrieval system without the written permission of the publisher except in the case of brief quotations embodied in critical articles and reviews.

iUniverse books may be ordered through booksellers or by contacting:

iUniverse
1663 Liberty Drive
Bloomington, IN 47403
www.iuniverse.com
1-800-Authors (1-800-288-4677)

Because of the dynamic nature of the Internet, any web addresses or links contained in this book may have changed since publication and may no longer be valid. The views expressed in this work are solely those of the author and do not necessarily reflect the views of the publisher, and the publisher hereby disclaims any responsibility for them.

Any people depicted in stock imagery provided by Thinkstock are models, and such images are being used for illustrative purposes only.

Certain stock imagery © Thinkstock.

ISBN: 978-1-4759-6699-2 (sc)
ISBN: 978-1-4759-6701-2 (e)
ISBN: 978-1-4759-6700-5 (hc)

Library of Congress Control Number: 2012923557

Printed in the United States of America

iUniverse rev. date: 03/12/2013

Preface –

In any given country or potentate, there is a ruler; be it king or queen, prime minister or president. He or she exercises rule, imposing or enforcing laws, seeing to the health and well-being of those over whom they rule. But on the Island of Manhattan, no such single man or woman holds such sway, though many seem to think they do. That the Island's two-legged inhabitants presume to have control over the goings-on there, presume to be the masters of their domain, would be terrible arrogance – if these humans weren't so charming and quaint. Manhattan's bipedal residents are free to *think* they control their destiny, but their ability to do so – to think that such an outlandish supposition is true – is solely due to the grace and charity of those who *really* run Manhattan: the creatures commonly referred to as "man's best friend."

Oh, you sir, or ma'am on the other end of the leash, if you only knew. *If you only knew.*

CHAPTER ONE –

In which our Hero, the Worldly McMurray, Is Taught Something about the World

McMurray stretched his sturdy limbs and let out a contented half-sigh, half-growl. Oh, but the sun felt *so* good. He lay drowsily on the ground, basking in the heat of the sunlit sidewalk. Although he preferred to rest on his side, he soon rolled onto his back so as to allow the warm, morning breeze to tickle his ample belly hairs. Then, as he always did after a good rest, he extended his four legs and turned over until he was standing on them, and shook out his full, reddish-brown coat of hair.

"Now, *that* was a nice little catnap," McMurray chuckled to himself.

Catnap. What a funny thing for McMurray to take pleasure in. After all, McMurray was a dog. And not just any dog – McMurray was a *dog's* dog. If McMurray's pedigree were to be officially labeled, (and it had been in so far as a mutt's can be), he would be deemed a Labrador–German shepherd mix. But a good deal of other breeds had been added to his lineage throughout the years, including Irish setter, which explained his name. It was the terrier in McMurray which was responsible for his relatively small stature.

Just as humans sometimes blame their relatives for what they perceive to be their less than desirable traits, McMurray possessed characteristics which he found less than appealing. He couldn't resist frequently stopping to admire the reflection of his wavy, lustrous coat in store windows, and the way his shaggy tail curled ever so delicately at the tip. But whenever he did he was reminded of how he hated his pointy ears. Then again, he conceded, he did have excellent hearing. And his black nose, while often too wet and shiny for his taste, did provide him with a more heightened sense of smell than others possessed. It was McMurray's stature which he resented most – that bit of terrier in him which had given him shorter legs than a dog as sophisticated as he should possess. They weren't overly short, per se, but sometimes when he saw a purebred German shepherd walk by, tall and regal, he recognized his ears, and wished he had also inherited those long, lean legs.

The stockier legs McMurray did inherit had served him well during his nearly eight years in the world. While he saw other dogs his age being wheeled down the sidewalk in manmade contraptions designed to compensate for bad hips and weak backs, McMurray still had a bounce in his step – and a growl at the ready. He'd been on his own for a long time, and in those years he had heard and seen it all.

McMurray was born on the streets, so to speak, although literally speaking he was born in a basement. His mother did an admirable job of fending for him and his five siblings. She had carved out a nice little corner of the world for them in the crowded cellar of a brownstone on Manhattan's Upper West Side. The homeowners, during a mad spat of redecorating, had tossed a treasure trove of unwanted items down there, most of which were in good condition – rolled up carpets, boxes of old curtains, outdated children's toys. That basement held everything a pup needed to stay warm and entertained. There was even a leaky pipe which provided plenty of drinking water.

McMurray's mother was able to come and go as she pleased, having figured out how to push open and then reclose an old basement window that led to a discrete, concrete staircase – which in turn led to the narrow alley between their building and the next. In this alley, a great deal of perfectly tasty garbage was stored for pick-up in rather flimsy containers.

It bears repeating that this was the Upper West Side of Manhattan. While in places its population represented humans from varied walks of life, the brownstones on the street where McMurray was born housed not multiple families, but single, privileged ones. These families had very nice things, and ate very fine food. Luckily, they didn't eat a lot of it.

Once McMurray and his siblings were weaned, their mother, who was overprotective and not comfortable allowing her pups to venture outside just yet, would journey up to the alley and return bearing discarded food from some of Manhattan's best restaurants. At a very young age, McMurray developed a taste for medium rare filet mignon, pecan crusted brook trout, and pasta carbonara. Every Friday night, the people whose basement McMurray and his family inhabited dined on high-quality Chinese take-out. And every Saturday morning, McMurray enjoyed his favorite dish – moo shuu pork. Luckily, their "host" family didn't seem to believe in leftovers.

As her pups grew, McMurray's mother had to face the fact that she couldn't keep them in the basement forever. As spacious as it was, there wasn't much light down there, and her offspring were getting curious about the world outside. Even though they knew they shouldn't make a sound, for fear of getting evicted, sometimes they couldn't contain their youthful barks when she returned from the alley. They yapped at her excitedly, begging to learn what lay beyond the chalky brick walls which contained them.

McMurray's mother was also getting antsy. Since she had given birth to her pups, she had confined herself to the basement and the alley above. She was afraid that if she ventured further, something might happen to her and she would be separated from her boys. She was, after all, a runaway. The people with whom she'd been living, who "owned" her, had no interest in taking care of a litter of puppies. Before she took up residence with them, she'd lived with a woman her new owners called "grandma," but whom McMurray's mother knew as Nanny. Nanny called McMurray's mother Honey – the new people referred to her as "that dog."

"I can't believe Grandma made us promise to take care of *that dog* without telling us she's pregnant!" the female shouted.

"That's our out then. We promised we'd take care of one mutt, not a litter of 'em. As soon as they're born, we'll drop 'em off at the shelter," the male told her.

"But the cost!" The female was always talking about how much things cost.

"Grandma left us a lot of money for that dog. There's plenty to cover the vet bills and we'll still have some cash left over for us." The male always found a way to pay for things.

McMurray's mother knew her situation was dire. Even taking her puppies out of the equation, she had no desire to stay with *those people*, as she referred to them. Nanny had been kind to her, although she'd become very absentminded toward the end, forgetting to put food in the dog bowl. And Nanny had grown very thin, apparently forgetting to feed herself as well.

McMurray's mother had taken to wandering the Upper West Side at night, after Nanny fell asleep. She learned where the best, most accessible food in the neighborhood was – not outside restaurants, as some might think. The people who owned restaurants were concerned about their bottom line.

Even at the nicer places, they kept the food a while, until it was about to turn and they *had* to toss it. Then they locked it in dumpsters out back, to keep the rats at a minimum.

But the people who ate at these restaurants... they were not nearly as concerned about money, it seemed. They ate out almost daily, and then casually tossed their succulent leftovers in trash cans in the alleys between their homes. Some people stored the cans in bins which were hard to get to, but others were much more careless. McMurray's mother quickly learned who the cavalier residents of the Upper West Side were.

She'd had help. It didn't take McMurray's mother long to come across others like her. Some dogs she met were homeless in the traditional sense – meaning they weren't kept by humans. Others were dissatisfied with their places of residence, and those with whom they resided, and were prone to escape. And then there were those like McMurray's mother, who were on the street because they had to be.

Although she learned a lot from them, McMurray's mother didn't like all the dogs she met at night – some she was downright afraid of. She came across some mean mutts whose bite was every bit as bad as their bark, who would follow her as she searched for food, then tackle her and steal what she'd retrieved. Dealing with these dogs made it easy for her to return to the safety of Nanny's rent controlled apartment each day just before sunrise.

Then she met McMurray's father. He was, of all things, a purebred – a gorgeous Irish setter. Most dogs roaming the streets were mutts like her. She was flattered when this meticulously groomed creature took an interest in her, a dog with no papers, who began her life in a shelter, not with a breeder. Not only did this Irish setter have one fancy home, he had two. On the weekends, the people with whom he lived took him to their residence in the country, where he was able to run free through the woods and hunt wild game. He found it painful to return to Manhattan every Sunday night, where he was only permitted outside on a leash, and only twice a day at that. So he took matters into his own paws and made a break for it as often as possible.

The people with whom McMurray's father lived were very attached to him. It bothered them that he got out so much without their permission. They took him to be examined by a man in a white coat, who wasn't like a regular veterinarian in that he talked to the people with whom McMurray's father lived more than he poked and prodded him. Then he asked to be alone with McMurray's father.

The man in the white coat spoke nonsense to him, but in very soothing tones. He felt his muscles for tension, and rubbed the tips of his long ears. It was all very relaxing, but McMurray's father decided this man was one of the loonier humans, not to be taken at all seriously. That was, until he issued his diagnosis.

"I believe," the man in the white coat said to the people with whom McMurray's father lived, "that your weekends in the country have spoiled Paddy. There is a longing, a sadness in his eyes that I have seen before in similar cases. The fact is it would be less stressful for all of you if Paddy remained at your home in Larchmont for the duration. Is that possible?"

It was indeed, for the Larchmont house was occupied at all times by a grumpy, older man whom everyone called Uncle Jake. Uncle Jake seemed to be happy only when he was outside shooting things. This suited McMurray's father just fine, as long as he could be outside with him. He told McMurray's mother so, the last time he saw her. She handled the news stoically. If this had been the decision of the humans, well, then there might have been reason for yelping and carrying on. But this is what McMurray's father had wanted, and his mother could do nothing except be happy for him.

About a week after McMurray's father departed for his new permanent home in the country, McMurray's mother found herself on a walk with Nanny after dark, a very unusual occurrence. McMurray's mother allowed herself to be put on a leash because she knew that was the law of the land, and a life with Nanny was preferable to one in the shelter from which Nanny rescued her three years prior, when she was five months old. McMurray's mother had seen more than she'd ever wanted to in that shelter. She felt fortunate that Nanny took her in when she did. Puppies had a chance, but older dogs... McMurray's mother couldn't bear to think about what happened to the older dogs. So she acquiesced, and donned a leash when she had to. Besides, Nanny wasn't exactly a task master.

"I don't know if I'm walking you, Honey, or if you're walking me!" Nanny frequently exclaimed when they were out together.

McMurray's mother knew – she was the one in charge. But on this one off night, things went terribly wrong. For starters, although Nanny was wearing her nightgown, she didn't seem to realize she should be in bed.

"Come on, Honey. Time to go to the store. We're out of milk! And I need to get the paper. I don't remember the last time I read the paper."

The newspaper was delivered every day. McMurray's mother brought one in every morning when she returned home from foraging, and piles of newspapers lay untouched around the apartment. Against her better judgment, McMurray's mother didn't resist when Nanny clipped the leash to her collar. *This is part of the deal*, she thought to herself. *She gives me a warm place to stay, I protect her.*

McMurray's mother led Nanny to the corner, hoping she would realize that the market was closed and turn back. Instead, Nanny, who had not put a coat on over her nightgown even though it was early November, said, "Let's go to the Duane Reade!"

Nanny started tugging at McMurray's mother's leash. "Come on, Honey! Let's go! Be a good girl now."

McMurray's mother didn't have to move – she had the

strength her German shepherd and Labrador lineage gave her, and the agility of an Airedale terrier, although she still wasn't certain how that breed got in the mix. But she didn't want to leave Nanny on her own; more than obligated to her, she felt almost maternal toward this old human. Nanny just seemed so lost.

So McMurray's mother followed Nanny across the street, against the light, with horns honking and cars swerving in their wake. Duane Reade wasn't a restaurant, so McMurray's mother had no reason to be familiar with the chain – she had no idea where one was. She tried to lead the old woman back to the apartment, but Nanny was growing very agitated.

"The Woolworth's was right here! Right here!" she shouted, pointing at a bank.

Passersby, although few and far between in that neighborhood at that hour, were staring, but not one stopped. McMurray's mother was confused … "I thought we were going to Duane Reade," she said to herself. "What's Woolworth's?"

Then Nanny started crying. "Hank! I want Hank!" she wailed. McMurray's mother knew that Hank was the human who appeared with Nanny in many of the photographs in the apartment. Nanny told Honey about him sometimes. More and more, Nanny spoke to Hank as if he was in the room for real, and not just in a picture.

McMurray's mother didn't know what to do. She sat down and waited patiently for Nanny's tantrum to pass. Then Nanny sat down as well. McMurray's mother walked over and licked Nanny's face, hoping the slobber would snap her back into reality.

"Good girl, Maggie. Good girl," Nanny said softly, patting McMurray's mother's thick, tan coat.

Maggie was the cocker spaniel Nanny had when she was a little girl; she talked about her sometimes, but more often lately. And that's when the policemen found them, sitting on the cold cement steps of the Chase bank that Nanny kept insisting should be a Woolworth's, Nanny half frozen in her see-through nightgown, gently petting a dog she called Maggie.

When McMurray's mother was brought to the shelter later that night by Animal Control, "Maggie" was the name they put on her cage. The humans seemed to take pity on her because of the circumstances in which she was taken in – loyally caring for an old lady with severe dementia. They stroked her and told her what a good girl she was.

McMurray's mother, in turn, took pity on the humans for being so easily suckered in by this sob story, and decided to respond when they called her Maggie. It didn't matter to her. Before she'd been named Honey, she'd been dubbed Suzy Q by the shelter Nanny got her from. She believed the only name that should mean anything is the one your real mother gave you, if you were a lucky enough mutt to know it. She wasn't.

McMurray's mother spent one full day and another night in the shelter, trying to resign herself to her fate as a prisoner. She couldn't, so she focused on her chances of getting out. She was almost four, but could probably pass for two. And she was attractive in a unique sort of way, except for her oddly shaped nose, courtesy of that pesky Airedale. But it turns out her fate was not sealed. The next morning, the people who called Nanny "grandma," whom McMurray's mother recognized from photographs but had never met, came and picked her up.

McMurray's mother would never lay her big, dark eyes on Nanny again, but the old woman had seen to it that her Honey would be taken care of. McMurray's mother was genuinely touched by the gesture, even though it left her in the hands of two humans with less scruples than a couple of hungry junkyard dogs. After only a few weeks with them, it became apparent that McMurray's mother was going to be a mother, something she herself had not realized. Nanny had promised, when she adopted McMurray's mother as a puppy, that she'd have her fixed – she never did. The humans to whom

Nanny had bequeathed her Honey soon initiated their heartless conversations about getting rid of the puppies. And that is when McMurray's mother made up her mind to escape.

One night, when the humans had a large group of people over to listen to loud music and chug beverages out of aluminum cans, McMurray's mother saw her chance. Everyone was going out on the fire escape to do something or other, which meant that even though it was freezing the window was open. When no one was looking, McMurray's mother jumped through the window and onto the green, metal landing outside. They were only on the second floor, so she simply had to climb down the ladder as far as she could, then drop the few feet to the alley below.

Since she was already familiar with the Upper West Side, it didn't take McMurray's mother long to figure out where she would go. She had found an excellent source of fine cuisine on West 76th Street, and the last time she was there noticed that a very unsecure window would easily allow her entrance to the house from which those delectable leftovers came.

McMurray's mother ran there as fast as she could – it was only a few blocks down and three avenues over – and hopped the gate into the alley next to the house. She wandered down the almost hidden stairs, which were badly deteriorated from age, to the basement door. The door itself was in terrible shape and as a result boarded up. The window next to it, which was just a foot from the ground, was completely neglected, the wood around the frame mildewed and rotten. McMurray's mother gently pushed the frosted glass pane open with her nose, just enough to get a good look inside.

The basement was packed with almost all the comforts of a human home, except, mercifully, there were no humans. She pushed the window open the rest of the way and jumped in, landing on a dresser which had been conveniently placed below, and then closed the window by skillfully maneuvering the inside handle with her strong jaw.

Humans, McMurray's mother thought. *So simple. So trusting.*

There, undisturbed, she prepared for the arrival of her puppies, making a nest out of a castoff Ralph Lauren bedspread. She gave birth around the time humans refer to as the New Year, to five beautiful little creatures – all boys, but with different color coats, and different shaped noses and ears. *Ah, the beauty of being a mutt!* she thought, staring down at her unique brood. One in particular stood out, with his reddish coat so much like his father's. She named him McMurray, in deference to his Irish heritage and an unfortunate old dog who had been very kind to her at the shelter when she was a pup.

Despite this show of sentimentality in naming him, McMurray's mother taught him early on that a smart dog doesn't grow attached to things, especially not human things – especially not humans.

"I saw it when I was in the shelter," she whispered to her pups at night. "Dogs whose people had left them, who were so sad and lost they couldn't bring themselves to eat. Remember, you *use* people, you don't need them.

"Yes, there are nice ones who love you and treat you well, but even then, it's not without a price. They always want something in return. Loyalty. Companionship. Tricks. No, even at its best, it's a relationship of give and take. Always make sure you're taking more than you're giving – just don't ever let the humans know it. Roll over every now and then, extend your paw, if it gets you a place at a well-stocked table."

She also warned McMurray and his siblings about the danger of becoming too attached to other dogs.

"It can be helpful to run in a pack," McMurray's mother told them, "but if you choose to do so, you need to remember your place, more so than with the humans. Humans can be fooled into thinking they're in charge, but an alpha dog *knows* he's in charge. Manhattan, it's not like the wild lands our ancestors knew. It's easy to lose your freedom here, and not just to a leash. You need to know how to look after yourselves, just in case you end up alone."

During their quiet days in the basement, she told them her life story, and all that she had learned from her experiences. The pups listened intently, soaking up the information, eagerly awaiting the day they would be grown and able to use it. No one ever disturbed them down there. Because the stairs to the alley were in such poor condition, the garbage was taken out the service entrance in the front of the house. The fuse boxes, hot water heater, furnace and other important devices were in a room on the other side of the vast basement. The pups heard humans on the stairs every now and then, and caught glimpses of their legs passing outside the windows, but they never actually saw one.

For her part, McMurray's mother did her best to keep any trace of her brood to a minimum. The pups were quickly paper trained, using the hundreds of copies of The New York Times that had made their way down to the basement. If they ever ran out of those, there were stacks of LIFE magazines. *It's fortunate that Manhattanites like to horde paper*, McMurray's mother thought.

She would carefully collect the soiled pages and dispose of them in the garbage when she went to forage at night. This got to be a more tedious task as the pups grew. *Besides*, she acknowledged to herself, *a proper dog doesn't do his business indoors!*

Finally, when her pups were about 11 weeks old, she decided it was time to take them outside, and really teach them something about the world. It was close to the official beginning of spring the night she carefully helped the pups climb the dresser and out the window, into the alley, where they stared up at the stars for the very first time. The air still had a chill in it; it was just the right temperature in which to catch a ripe scent. McMurray's mother watched proudly as her boys lifted their noses to the air, and took in the many smells of

Manhattan. She showed them the garbage bin from which they had been dining, which they immediately wanted to relieve themselves on.

"Good instinct, boys," she said, "but it's bad manners – a tree or rock will do much better. Let's go to the park."

The pups were small enough to squeeze themselves under the alley gate, and McMurray's mother jumped over the way she used to. *It does feel good to be out again*, she thought, as she landed heavily on the sidewalk.

The park, of course, was Central Park. They were only blocks from it. There wasn't a lot of nightlife with which to contend, especially this late, but still the family had to be careful, traveling quietly in the shadows. And they had to cross the street. McMurray's mother taught the boys to not just look, but listen, for traffic.

"Cab drivers come out of nowhere!" she warned. "Use your ears."

She felt better, safer when she got them to the park. The pups reveled in the feel of the grass beneath the soft pads of their paws, the scent of the grass, and the mystery that lay behind every bush. Over the course of several weeks, they covered most of the expanse of the park – the North Meadow, the Reservoir, the Great Lawn, the Sheep Meadow.

"It's best," McMurray's mother told her sons, "to stay away from the East Side. There are more places over there for humans. Big buildings with important things hanging on their walls. They like to go there and look – no dogs allowed."

The family loved their nightly adventures. McMurray's mother tried to wear them out, so they slept most of the day and didn't mind being cooped up so much. She caught McMurray staring out the window often, daydreaming, longing for the sunlight. *Just like his father*, she thought.

She told them they could go out during the day when they were experienced enough to live without her. The day they were without their mother was not something the pups liked to think about, although they knew it was inevitable. It was a fact of every dog's life. Then fate intervened and hastened that inevitability.

One night, toward the end of April, there was an unexpected cold snap, a frost. The pups were out in Central Park with their mother, getting used to the feel of ice on their paws. They ran and slid, rolling over each other, playing as if they didn't have a care in the world. It was hard for their mother to get them to return home. When they did, they found the basement they had lived in for almost four months flooded with water.

It was dangerous to go inside, but just as dangerous to be outside in the soon to be light of day. McMurray's mother decided they should go in and rest on top of the old furniture that was scattered against the walls, while she thought of somewhere they would be safe. And they did just that, seeking refuge on the dresser, some old book shelves, and a three-legged breakfront, while their "host" family's riff raff floated by below, in water that was getting higher by the minute. Out of nowhere, they heard the heavy thud of footsteps on the stairs, and a bright circle of light was visible through the doorway.

"Gotta be a burst pipe." It was a man's voice. "I'm shuttin' off the water. They're lucky it didn't hit the electrical."

"How much we gonna get an hour for fixing this mess? The sun's barely up." This was spoken by a different voice, another man. They were in the other part of the basement.

"Enough, so stop your whinin'. There, that oughta do it. Water's off."

Then the footsteps hit the stairs again.

"Shouldn't we check out the damage while we're down here?"

"Yeah, sure, I guess."

And suddenly a beam of light was shining through the doorway which separated the important part of the basement from the one McMurray and his family occupied.

"These old houses, I swear." It was the first man – his voice was gruffer, more mean sounding. "Get a load of all the junk they got down here."

The two men were standing side by side, wearing rubber boots that went up to their thighs. Each of them was holding a flashlight.

The mean sounding man put a spotlight on McMurray's mother, sitting on the dresser beneath the window with one of her pups. The other man turned his light on the bookshelf which was standing to the right, on top of which two of McMurray's brothers were huddled close. Then the light moved to the other side of the dresser, where it found McMurray, sitting with the fourth of his brothers on the wobbly breakfront.

"Holy geez! What the heck is this? An animal refuge?"

"Hey, how's it looking down there? You guys okay?"

"Uh, Mr. Chumpski, are you aware you got a bunch of dogs down here?"

"What?"

"You got a family of canines hiding out down here!"

McMurray's mother had opened the window. The sun was just coming up. She nudged the pup sitting with her outside. "Run!" she barked at him.

She looked helplessly at her other boys, who were yelping at the two intruders. "Come to me!" she barked.

The pups on the book shelf began to make their mother, while McMurray and his other brother waited their turn. There wasn't room for all of them on the sagging, soggy dresser. McMurray's mother hurried the process along, grabbing one of her pups by the fleshy part of his neck with her mouth, then pushing him out the window. She did this with the other pup then turned her attention to McMurray and his brother. Meanwhile, the two men retreated upstairs.

The breakfront wasn't stable. It wobbled under McMurray and his brother when they moved to jump onto the dresser. Their mother reached over to grab them by the nape of their neck, the way she had their brothers, but the most she could do was steady them to keep them from falling into the cold water below. Hopefully, if they did fall, instinct would take over; it hadn't yet been warm enough to teach them to swim. And all this time, McMurray's mother was thinking about her pups outside, wondering if they had gotten away, wondering where they would go.

Many minutes had passed by the time McMurray's mother was able to get all her boys out of the basement. By the time she ascended herself, her legs were trembling with fear. On the one paw, she would be relieved if her pups escaped. On the other, she would be worried sick, not knowing what became of them. With great trepidation, she stepped out into the light. There she saw Mr. Chumpski and his wife and their two children, whom she had seen many times from afar entering and leaving their house, cradling and cooing at her pups.

McMurray's mother barked, trying not to sound too ferocious, walking a fine line between defending her young and getting sacked by Animal Control. She knew if she bit anyone, it was all over. They would put her down. She definitely wouldn't be able to protect her pups then. Her poor pups; they had never been touched by humans before. *What if they like it too much?* She wondered. *Have I taught them well enough?*

McMurray's mother barked until Animal Control arrived. The family handed the pups over to the humans in uniform, who transferred them into two crates. Their mother was loaded into the van separately. She was fine with the fact that the humans faced her crate away from her boys – at least they would not be able to see the terrible sadness in her eyes.

CHAPTER TWO –

McMurray Strikes Out on His Own

McMurray didn't see his mother's eyes again. The family was brought to the same shelter, but the puppies were taken to one room, their mother to another. It was all very confusing for the boys. They knew what the shelter was, but they had no idea what was going to happen next. They certainly were not lacking for attention.

"You're so cute. Yes you are! Yes you are!"

A young woman was leaning over the pups, speaking in a very high-pitched voice that came close to hurting their ears. They had been transferred to a large pen, and were all together again.

"Let me see your belly. Let me see!" the young woman continued, prodding the boys onto their backs and giving each of their bellies a solid rub.

"All boys!" she confirmed to another young woman standing behind her with a clipboard. "None of them are fixed. It's hard to tell because they're mutts, but I don't think they're six months old yet.

"What kind of mutts do you think they are?"

"Not sure. The mother is definitely a Labrador-German

shepherd mix. Just write that down. They're going to need the standard blood work, and assuming that all comes back okay, the usual shots. For now, let's keep them in quarantine."

"Got it."

Then the two women turned out the lights and left the room. The pups had been provided with several bowls of something they could not identify, but they assumed it was supposed to be food since it was next to bowls of water. They were given dense, hard pillows and scratchy blankets to lie on. Instead, they curled up on top of each other, finding solace in each other's warmth and the sound of each other's fast, steady heartbeats. They missed their mother, but she had trained them well. They knew what she would want them to do – forget about her, and look out for themselves.

Only they weren't quite sure how to do that. The pups were having a very hard time figuring out whether the humans were trying to help them or hurt them. Lots of things they did to them definitely hurt, but they did them while speaking in soft, gentle tones, telling them how adorable they were, what good boys. "We're going to make you strong and healthy," they said. The pups had always thought they were.

Then the day came when they were taken out of quarantine and put in a big room with many other dogs. The concrete walls were lined with cages, and the sound of barking reverberated throughout the room. They didn't recognize their mother's bark among the many they heard, although they listened carefully for it. The pups were happy that at least they were still all together, in one large pen.

Humans would come by and look at them through the bars, mostly humans with children.

"I like that one!" little boys and girls would shout, sticking their fingers through the metal to point.

"Sweetie, don't do that! Never put your hand in a strange animal's cage. Wait till he comes to you."

Then the children would crouch down and wait. Eventually,

in hopes that it would make them go away, one of McMurray's brothers would go over and give the children a pity lick. Never McMurray though. He had no interest in playing their game.

One day, about a month after they arrived, the young woman with the clipboard came and took two of McMurray's brothers away – *two* at once. They never returned. Sometimes, people took the pups out to play, but in the past they had all always come back. The next week, another of the brother's went missing. A week later, yet another. And then there was just McMurray. He was moved from the pen to a small cage, where he stayed by himself for another two weeks. He ate the awful pellets they gave him which they referred to as "breakfast" and "dinner." He drank their water. He did his business outside like a "good boy." But it was all just to buy time until he could come up with a plan to escape.

Then, out of nowhere, escape came to McMurray. Two weeks after his last brother went missing he was visited by two humans and their little boy. McMurray did his best to seem disinterested, but in his cramped cage there was nowhere to go. He turned so his behind was in their faces; for some reason this made the little boy laugh uncontrollably.

"I like this one, Daddy!" the child screamed. "Mommy, I want this one!"

"He seems a little standoffish, sweetheart," his mother said. "Can we take him out to the run?"

"Sure you can. Remember, most of these animals have been traumatized so it might take them a while to warm up to you. We offer free training classes, to help them acclimate to life with a family." It was that pesky young woman with the clipboard again.

I had a family, McMurray thought.

He let them put a leash on him and take him outside. It was so much warmer now than it had been the morning he and his family were brought to the shelter. McMurray immediately lay down in the sunshine, and rolled over on his back.

"See, Daddy – he's funny! I bet I can teach him to do tricks."

"He's had all his shots?" the mother asked.

Have I ever! McMurray answered silently.

"Yes. He tested negative for worms, heartworm, Distemper – clean bill of health. The only thing is you'll need to bring him back in about a month to be fixed. He's still too young. Or you can have it done at your own vet, of course. But we do require that everyone who adopts from us gets their pet fixed. You have to sign something."

"Of course. Well, Tommy – what do you think? You want to see some other puppies?"

Say yes, say yes, say yes, McMurray wished to himself.

"Nope, Daddy. This is my dog. This is Barkley."

"Isn't that cute? Barkley Farber! You're a very clever boy, Tommy," his mother told him.

Barkley? Seriously? My name is McMurray! It's McMurray, I tell ya!

McMurray began barking and jumping up and down with great enthusiasm, trying to get the Farbers to understand that they were making a mistake.

"See, he loves his new name!" the woman with the clipboard said, missing the point.

"You call him Erik now?" Mrs. Farber asked.

"Yes, like Erik the Red, because his coat is kind of red. But he's never answered to it."

Darn right I haven't. Because my name is McMurray!

Tommy was patting McMurray's head, trying to calm the pup down. "When can we take him home?"

"Well, your parents filled out the required paperwork last month, and you've passed the home visit, so there's just the matter of the adoption fee and you're set. You can take Barkley home today!" the woman said, reviewing her notes.

Her words rendered McMurray silent. *So this is what happened to my brothers,* he thought.

Within 30 minutes, McMurray was in the back of a Volvo station wagon; according to the chit chat he overheard, he was heading to a placed called Brooklyn. He wondered if Brooklyn was anywhere near Central Park. McMurray looked intently out the window, but none of the scenery whizzing by seemed familiar. This was only his second time in a motor vehicle – the first being the ride he took in the Animal Control van. He found the motion somewhat soothing, but any feelings of comfort he experienced were cancelled out by feelings of anxiety; after all, he didn't know where he was going, or who was taking him there. *Who are these people named Farber?* he wondered.

McMurray turned his attention from the window to study the humans who had taken him from the shelter. The Farbers had carefully put down a towel and coaxed him into the car, positioning him behind the driver's seat.

"Stay, Barkley. Stay. We don't have your harness or crate," Mr. Farber told him. "We didn't expect to be taking you home so soon!"

Then they belted the boy in next to him. McMurray understood the words they were speaking, but due to his lack of familiarity with humans and human things, he didn't know what many of them meant. "I don't like the sound of this thing called harness," he said to himself. "Seems like a fancy word for leash to me."

Mr. Farber was up front, steering the car. From where he sat, the only part of Mr. Farber which McMurray had a decent view of was the back of his head. *He could certainly use some more fur up there*, the pup thought, checking to see if he could make out his reflection in Mr. Farber's shiny bald spot.

McMurray had a better view of Mrs. Farber, who was sitting next to her husband in the passenger's seat. She was a small woman, with dark, bouncy curls on her head which McMurray admired very much. *She looks pleasant enough*, he thought – although he was very distracted by the large, sparkly object she wore on her left hand. When she spoke (which was almost always), she frequently pointed at her husband.

"I told your sister that Macy's was never going to take those shoes back!" she let Mr. Farber know, wagging the index finger of her left hand at him. And when she did, McMurray saw how the object on her other finger caught the sun's rays. Fascinated, he followed the bits of light it cast on the car's interior.

"Whatcha lookin' at boy?" the child next to him asked.

McMurray stared at the smallest of the three Farbers. He could see that under the boy's cap were curls similar to his mother's, but they were a little lighter in color and much shorter. The child was missing two front teeth – one on the top and one on the bottom – but that didn't stop him from chewing frantically on a big gob of something pink. *Maybe that's why he's so loud*, McMurray thought. *It must be hard to talk with his mouth so full.*

"You're gonna like your new home, Barkley," the child screamed in his ear, while patting the top of McMurray's head with his sticky hands. McMurray didn't like the shouting or the touching one bit. He whimpered loudly.

"You doin' okay back there, buddy?" Mr. Farber asked.

"It's okay Barkley," Mrs. Farber tried to reassure him. "We're going to take good care of you. Not like your sister's family with that out of control Labradoodle of theirs. I'm telling you Dan, that dog is going to ruin every piece of carpet in their house." Again, she was wagging her finger.

McMurray was no longer so entertained by the pieces of light cast by the sparkly thing. He continued to whimper for the duration of the ride to Brooklyn. He whimpered all afternoon as the Farbers got him settled in their home and all through the night in his crate in the laundry room. He was pretty sure the Farbers couldn't hear him from there, since they were sleeping two floors above; still, he wasn't doing it for attention or effect. He was a genuinely miserable pup.

In the morning, he completely neglected his so-called food, even though Mrs. Farber implored him to eat it.

"Leave it. He'll eat it when he gets hungry," Mr. Farber said.

McMurray didn't eat it though. At dinner, Mrs. Farber threw it out and gave him fresh pellets covered in brown water. It was just as unappealing as it had been at breakfast. McMurray would have none of it. The next morning, it was still there, untouched, and looking more unpalatable than ever.

"Do you think he'd eat some eggs?"

"Betsy, please! He's a dog! We can't start giving him people food his second day here."

"He's gonna starve! Barkley's gonna starve!" the boy chimed in.

"He's not going to starve. He'll eat when he's hungry."

"Dan, he has to be hungry. Let's just try to give him some scrambled eggs."

"Fine, do what you want. I'm late for work."

Mr. Farber left, and Mrs. Farber made Tommy and McMurray scrambled eggs. She put McMurray's portion in the refrigerator a moment to let them cool, thinking the pup wasn't smart enough not to eat something that would burn him. McMurray was offended by this, but as soon as he smelled the eggs cooking in the pan, his mouth had begun to salivate. He couldn't deny that he was in fact quite hungry. Mrs. Farber put a paper plate piled with eggs down in front of him. He sniffed it coyly. He licked the fluffy, yellow pillows of yolk.

"See Barkley, they're good. See," the boy prompted, shoveling a large forkful of eggs into his own mouth.

McMurray took a bite of the eggs, and then another, and then another. Before he knew it, he had devoured every bit of egg on the plate, and was licking the paper clean. He traveled with it across the slippery linoleum floor. Just as he was about to lose the plate under the refrigerator, he heard it – that horrible sound. The boy and Mrs. Farber were laughing. And they weren't just laughing, they were laughing *at him*.

Still, McMurray thought, *I got her to give me real food. Then again, I'm perfectly capable of foraging for my own food. I don't need these people!*

"Stop your laughing! Stop it!" he barked. "I can get my own darn eggs."

Again, he was totally misunderstood. Mrs. Farber bent down and kissed him on the nose. "Okay, I'll make you some more eggs, you poor dear. But just this once."

Mrs. Farber made McMurray eggs every morning for the next 28 mornings that she could call him her dog.

Mrs. Farber also allowed McMurray to sleep on Tommy's bed, to eat table scraps at dinner, and to spend a good deal of time at the local dog run. Still, as his mother had taught him, it was a tradeoff. For one, he had no choice but to answer to the name Barkley. These humans would simply not let that one slide. They would stand in front of him and say the word over and over again, "Barkley! Barkley! Look here, Barkley! Come here, Barkley!" until the pup's head was spinning. It was easier to just give in.

Also, Tommy was constantly imploring him to do tricks. Even Mrs. Farber, as easy a mark as she was, insisted that McMurray sit on command. He gave her that one – *threw her a bone*, so to speak. But the whole "give paw" thing was a little much. He couldn't understand why humans were so fascinated by this simple action. Tommy spent hours begging McMurray to give him his paw. The child was so earnest that McMurray felt it would be cruel to deny him.

"Here, here's my paw," he barked, extending his limb to the excited child. "You've earned it."

"That's a good boy!" Tommy praised, throwing his arms around McMurray's neck. "Here's a Nilla Wafer."

The child was much happier to receive the dog's paw than the dog was to receive a Nilla Wafer. But McMurray gave in to the human's demands enough to ward off any official training – no obedience school for Barkley, the wonder dog! But he could not overcome the matter of the harness.

How hated the harness. Every time they came at him with it, he ran. His assumption had been correct – it was just a different kind of leash. All the hip Brooklynites were using them; McMurray heard the humans so say at the dog run. It was supposedly a humane alternative to the choke collar, and it certainly sounded better to McMurray than something with the word "choke" in its name. Tommy frequently shouted that he was "choking" during meals. McMurray watched him cough and gasp, watched his eyes tear up and his face turn red. Then Mrs. Farber would rush over to pat him on his back, and force him to take some sips of water

"You eat too fast, Tommy. Chew your food!" Mrs. Farber would warn with that busy finger of hers.

"I couldn't breathe, Mommy! I could've died. I could've choked to death!"

If a choke collar could do to a dog what improperly chewed pieces of food could do to a human boy, McMurray certainly wanted no part of it. Still, the harness was humiliating. It was stifling. When he was wearing that harness, it was the only time McMurray truly felt he was owned by the Farbers; it was the only time he felt he was being submissive not because he chose to be, but because they were forcing him to be.

Yet he tolerated this for 28 days. Because when it came down to it, McMurray figured that as far as humans went, the Farbers were probably not much different than any other family that would've brought him home. After all, his mother had been through all this, and his brothers were probably going through it too. Being with the Farbers was definitely better than being at the shelter.

But then, on the 28th day came the final straw, the final burr in McMurray's paw. Mr. and Mrs. Farber wanted him to have an operation. Not just any operation, but one that would take away that which McMurray held very dear. It was bad enough that they took away his manhood figuratively every time they put him in a harness, but this, this "fixing" as they called it – it was just too much. McMurray had heard all about it in the shelter, and he wanted no part.

Living with the Farbers was better than living in the shelter, but it wasn't better than living freely, on the streets of Manhattan, as he'd done for the first four months of his life. He had to get his freedom back. He had heard Mr. and Mrs. Farber talking; they were taking him back to the shelter for the operation. McMurray supposed that the shelter was pretty close to the Upper West Side, since that's where Animal Control nabbed him. If he could somehow make a break for it between Brooklyn and the shelter, he could probably find his way back to Central Park.

Because of how well behaved he was during that first fateful drive with them, the Farbers hardly ever put McMurray's harness on when they were taking him in the car. They had one of the rarest commodities in all of New York City – a garage, attached to their house, in which they were able to park their car every night. They would let McMurray out to the garage through the basement, and he would jump right into the backseat as soon as they opened the car door.

Most of the time McMurray was just going along for the ride, not leaving the car again until he returned back at the Farbers' home, which meant no tethers necessary. The morning of the operation, all he had to do was jump in the car before the Farbers realized that this time he was going to need his harness. McMurray didn't consider this a difficult feat – the Farbers were usually distracted by something Tommy had or hadn't done. Getting rid of the collar with those telltale tags was something altogether more complicated. Luckily, the Farbers took care of that problem for him.

Mrs. Farber didn't want her precious baby Barkley (as she frequently called him) to go under the knife a dirty dog, so she endeavored to bathe him that morning. He hadn't enjoyed being bathed the two times Mrs. Farber had tried it before; she let the soap get in his eyes. But a bath meant she would take off his collar. So for this particular exercise in cleanliness, McMurray managed a bit more enthusiasm than usual. He let Mrs. Farber work up a good lather on his back with the horrible green shampoo that smelled very similar to the products with which she cleaned the tub. He even let her use her hair dryer on him afterward.

"You do have such a beautiful coat," she admired while she brushed him. McMurray barked and wagged his tail. Just as Mrs. Farber was finishing grooming him, he jumped off her lap and began to run through the house, barking excitedly. Then he ran to the basement door, waiting to be let out to the car.

"Do you think he knows where he's going?" Mrs. Farber asked her husband.

"If he did, I can't imagine he'd be so happy about it. Poor son of a gun."

"Well, he seems eager to go."

"Let's go then and get this over with. Tommy, come on! We're taking Barkley to get fixed now."

"Be right there, Dad!"

"Now, Tommy! And bring your new baseball glove so we can exchange it for a bigger one."

"I can't find it, Dad."

"I just bought it for you last night. How is it possible you lost it already?"

"I don't know."

"Where did you last have it?" Mrs. Farber stepped in.

"I don't know," Tommy said again.

"Let's go up to your room and try to find it."

"Betsy, we can't be late. If he lost his glove, I guess he doesn't play baseball this summer."

"Don't be ridiculous, Dan."

"I'm being ridiculous? The kid lost his glove in 12 hours, while he was sleeping."

Things went on like this for 10 more minutes. It was excruciating to listen to – Tommy lost at least three things a day – but it was a helpful distraction. With her attention turned to finding the baseball glove, Mrs. Farber would never remember that she hadn't put the dog collar back on the dog.

"We're going to be late! I'm going to the car!" Mr. Farber yelled. McMurray was still at the basement door, waiting to be let into the garage. When the door opened, he bounded to the car. "There you go boy," Mr. Farber said, opening the back door for him. "Poor son of a gun."

Two minutes later, Mrs. Farber and Tommy followed. Mrs. Farber had the collar and harness in hand. "I should really put this on," she said.

"When we get there. We're late. There's going to be traffic on the bridge."

"But…"

"Betsy, not now!"

That was the only time McMurray felt an ounce of affection for Mr. Farber. And he was right. There was traffic on the bridge, and all the way up the West Side Highway.

"You should've taken Hudson to 8th Avenue," Mrs. Farber said, her finger wagging.

"Betsy, please."

"I'm just saying…"

"I have to go to the bathroom," Tommy interrupted.

Here's my chance, McMurray thought.

"You're going to have to hold it, buddy. There's nowhere to stop."

"But Daddy, I have to go to the bathroom!"

"I heard you the first time Tommy, but there's nowhere to stop now."

"There's a gas station on 11th. We just need to turn off right here."

"Besty, gosh darn it!"

"What?"

"There's a gas station on 11ᵗʰ, Dad. I gotta go."

"Fine. Fine!"

Mr. Farber found his way to the gas station on 11ᵗʰ. His wife told him to take Tommy to the men's room. "In the meantime, I'll put Barkley's collar and harness on."

Tommy had left the back door open when he got out. Mrs. Farber was standing beside it on the passenger side, explaining to her husband about the collar and harness as he was on the way to the bathroom with their son. And while this was going on, McMurray was seizing his moment. He jumped from the back seat out the open door, into the gas station parking lot.

"Barkley, what are you doing, baby?" Mrs. Farber asked innocently.

McMurray took one last look at the woman who had essentially been a surrogate mother to him those past 28 days. *But really,* he thought, *I think I was more of a second child to you than you were a second mother to me.* And with that final realization, McMurray turned tail and ran as fast he could north. He was close to the park – he could feel it.

"Barkley!" Mrs. Farber screamed after him. "Dan! Dan, come quick! Barkley's run away!"

Because of McMurray's excellent hearing, he had to put a couple of blocks between himself and Mrs. Farber before her high-pitched wails faded into the sound of the traffic. He never once looked back, and he had no intention of ever doing so. But even the best laid plans of a savvy mutt like McMurray can go astray.

CHAPTER THREE –

Our Hero Learns it Takes all Kinds

MCMURRAY MADE IT TO Central Park just fine the day he liberated himself from the Farbers. During his travels, any time he thought people were looking at him suspiciously, he just sidled up to an elderly man or woman and pretended he was with them. This was a trick he would use often. He had noticed that humans were much more charitable to older people who didn't leash their dogs, letting the infraction go with just a stare, a shrug, or sometimes a shake of the head – as opposed to calling Animal Control.

On his own in the world, Mc Murray thrived. It gave him tremendous joy to run free through Central Park at night again, to make his way through the back alleys of Manhattan, finding much better fare in trash bins than he was served in the shelter, or even at the Farbers' – despite, in all fairness, Mrs. Farbers' ability to whip up some pretty delectable eggs.

McMurray felt the most free under the protective blanket of night, when the stores were closed and the streets on which they stood relatively empty. The parks were almost always blissfully free of humans after dark – at least of the kind of humans who gave a hoot about a stray dog. McMurray could usually find a warm, dry place to sleep when he needed one. He had a talent for predicting the weather; he could smell snow a full day before it fell, catch the scent of rain well in advance of it trickling down, and make out a thundercloud hours before it clapped.

But there were rare times when he was distracted and his powers failed him, leaving him vulnerable to a sudden shower. McMurray didn't mind getting rained on a couple of times a year. He was made of sturdy stock. His thick coat acted as it was meant to, and shielded him well from the elements. Besides, he could take a little cold, a little damp. It was a small price to pay for his freedom.

McMurray went back to the visit the basement on West 76th Street only once, the night after he escaped the Farbers. He thought maybe, just maybe, his mother and siblings had also been able to escape whoever had taken them in, and what better place to regroup than their old home? He had to satisfy his curiosity before he could truly move on. So when it was very late, and he was sure the humans who had hosted them would be asleep, he carefully made the trip to the alley which led to the basement where he was born.

McMurray was not yet a grown dog, but also wasn't a small pup anymore. He couldn't sneak under the alley's gate, and he had a heck of a time trying to jump over it. But McMurray was a clever dog, a thrifty dog. He saw that the Chumpskis' neighbors had piled some garbage on the curb, and among this garbage was something quite priceless to McMurray. He spied among the trash a beaten up wooden box, with two little drawers and of all things, a handle on top. He went over and picked it up by the handle; the box had been emptied of whatever contents it had held, and was reasonably light. McMurray placed the box under the gate, and used it as a stepstool – it lent him just enough height so that he could jump to the top of the gate and propel himself over.

He landed on the concrete below less than gracefully, but

unharmed. He looked around. The alley smelled the same. It looked the same. He walked over to the almost hidden staircase, which was still in a state of disrepair. The old door was still well boarded. But the window – the window had been completely sealed. The broken wooden frame had been replaced with a strong metal one, and the frosted pane of glass was now covered with wire and protected with bars. It seemed that the Chumpskis had learned their lesson. McMurray tried to peer inside, but the small light bulb the Chumpski's used to illuminate the alley wasn't much help, and the basement was completely dark.

"Even if my family did make it back here," McMurray said to himself, "they couldn't have gotten inside."

He stood next to the window for a few more moments, trying very hard not to be sad. His mother had endeavored to instill in his brothers and him a spirit of independence, knowing that a dog's life could be a much lonelier one than it seemed. And it was at that moment that McMurray realized he was, in fact, truly alone. His family was gone. He did not have nor did he want any humans to call him their own.

McMurray let out a long sigh, which contained just a hint of a whimper, and with that he said good-bye to his past, to his mother and brothers, and to the basement where he had been born. He slowly turned and walked back to the gate and stared up at it, his heavily lashed, brown eyes glowing with determination.

"I can do this," he told himself.

He backed up and took a flying leap toward the gate, managing to latch on to the top of it with his paws. He held on as tight as he could, and although it was a struggle, he was able to pull himself up and throw himself over to the ground below. He ran from the house on West 76th Street, barking loudly to commemorate his triumph over the gate, not caring if he woke the whole neighborhood, and especially not caring if he woke the Chumpskis. McMurray kept running until he reached Central Park. He resolved never to think about that basement or his family again. It was, he decided, beyond his control.

Despite the worldliness McMurray had achieved at such a young age, he still had much to learn. When it came to some things, McMurray was very capable of educating himself. He genuinely enjoyed people watching. During warm, sunny days, he would station himself at the feet of an elderly human who was resting in the park; he never had trouble finding someone sitting alone, although it was mostly old men, not women, populating the benches. Some individuals told him to "shoo" as soon as they saw him approach, but most accepted his company warmly, and fed him bits of sandwich, pieces of apple, or whatever simple food they had.

McMurray and the old man or woman he chose on any given day would watch children play, listen to mothers converse and reprimand their kids, count the number of times cyclists looped the bike path, and stare astounded at the tricks teenagers could do on things with wheels. Tommy Farber would often ride his bicycle to the dog run with him, but McMurray soon learned what rollerblades and skateboards were as well. Sometimes, visitors holding maps stopped at the bench to ask the old human for directions; McMurray always tried to help, but he was fairly certain no one understood him – tourists!

In this way, through openly spying on society, McMurray became intimately familiar with the ways of humans, with their habits and names for things. It helped that the older humans he used for cover had a tendency to talk to themselves, or at least say things out loud to no one in particular, especially when reading the newspaper. McMurray enjoyed hearing commentary about the goings on in the world – the high price of oil and a two bedroom walk-up in the East Village, the foibles of the humans' leaders, and the follies of their celebrities. Many of the elderly humans even spoke directly to McMurray.

"So, young fella – you sneak away for a walk too? Looking

for some fresh air, are you? Well, I can't blame you. It's hard being cooped up inside on a beautiful day like this."

McMurray found it interesting how almost all the older humans felt a kinship with him, assumed they had something in common. McMurray heard the word "projection" thrown around the playground often.

"My mother went on and on last night about how I can't let raising kids ruin my career. She insisted that I should go back to work. I told her to stop projecting her issues on to me. Just because she resented staying home with her kids, that doesn't mean I feel the same way about my life!"

McMurray thought that perhaps the older humans were projecting their feelings on to him, and that they must have felt cooped up wherever it was they were living. Some invited him home with them, but most just said, "See ya tomorrow, boy, God willing."

McMurray could tell these older humans were lonely, and perhaps a little sad. Even though they felt a connection to him, these were not the humans with whom McMurray felt a kinship. No, it wasn't the people who *sat* on benches he truly took to, but the ones who slept on them.

Through his careful observations, McMurray realized that there was a contingent of humans who, like him, made the streets of Manhattan their home. He watched them forage through trash, just as he did. He watched them stake out a dry, comfortable place in which to rest, the same as him. And he watched them take hand-outs from humans, just as he sometimes managed to do.

It was this business of human begging which fascinated McMurray, especially when he realized that some of the homeless people doing so had dogs at their side. One day, when he had been free for about six months, he decided to approach a mostly Labrador-looking mutt who was resting next to the shopping cart of a homeless man. McMurray waited until the man disappeared inside a nearby delicatessen, and then asked him about the practice of homeless dogs and humans living together.

"We're partners," the mutt explained. "The guys who panhandle with dogs get a bigger take."

"Panhandle? Take?" This was terminology McMurray hadn't heard before.

"Panhandle... you know, beg – but mostly for money. The take is what they bring in."

"How does money help you? You can't buy anything," McMurray pointed out.

"That's the beauty of the deal. My guy does the buyin' for me. Right now, he's inside that deli gettin' a corned beef on rye. This place has the best corned beef on the West Side."

"But does this man own you?" McMurray asked the mutt.

"He might think he does, but I look at it as more of a business arrangement. He only ties me up when people start makin' comments about Animal Control or whatever. Most of the time, I got free reign of the streets, just like him. He knows I ain't goin' nowhere, so long as he keeps feedin' me the good stuff. And you know, if he gets into any scrapes, I act all tough, do some protectin' to earn my stay through the lean times."

McMurray was fascinated. "How did you work out this arrangement?"

"I went lookin' for a guy who didn't seem to be doin' so well on his own, and when I found one, just started sleepin' next to him. Since his take increased with me there, he let me stay and share in the profits. I'd rather eat fresh food than leftovers any day. But don't you even think about stickin' round here and stealin' my racket. If you're interested in startin' your own business, do it somewhere else," the mutt warned. "We got this corner."

His entrepreneurial spirit aroused, McMurray decided to investigate further. He noticed that there were a number of panhandling teams on the streets by the park, streets which saw a lot of foot traffic, especially from tourists. It seemed that the best market may have been cornered, but McMurray was not that easily deterred. Although he generally shied away from the Upper East Side, he thought it might hold more promise. At sunset, being careful to stay away from the heavily traveled paths that bridged west and east, or to be more specific Central Park West and Fifth Avenue, McMurray made his way across the park, to the land of big buildings with important things hanging on their walls.

It was different on the East Side. Even at night, McMurray thought it seemed busier, less relaxed, even though there weren't many people on the streets. Maybe, he surmised, that was because they were all in the large number of taxi cabs he saw – many more than on the West Side. And their horns seemed to honk much louder and with greater frequency than those of West Side taxi cabs. McMurray noticed that while on the West Side humans tended to wander, on the East Side, everyone seemed to have a place where they needed to be, and they needed to get there very quickly. It was all just so tidy.

"It's not going to be easy to find a homeless man over here," he said, almost ready to give up and head back. He knew the East Side was no place for an unleashed dog. But before turning tail, he meandered north, and then a bit further east – and there, on Third Avenue, providence struck. McMurray happened upon a very inviting Chinese restaurant.

He smelled the establishment before he saw it. The scent of fried Chinese delicacies caused a string of saliva to drip from his jowls. Suddenly, he was famished. He licked his chops. There was no shortage of Chinese restaurants in Manhattan, but accessing their leftovers wasn't always easy. McMurray saw an alley nearby, and was just about to investigate whether it contained any of the restaurant's trash, when he felt something swipe at him from behind.

"Get out of here you dang mutt!" a stranger's voice ordered.

McMurray quickly turned around. "Are you speaking to me?" he barked.

The man in front of him was wielding a fly swatter. He was unshaven with wild, curly hair and his clothes, like his skin, were quite wrinkled. Despite his need for a good grooming, he was fairly clean, although he was clutching a plastic shopping bag that appeared to be full of junk. He had a large object strapped to his back.

"I said get!" he shouted, flailing the fly swatter through the air.

Instead of trying to reason with the man, McMurray decided to sit down and simply hold his ground. The man stared at McMurray – his eyes were very dark, while the bushy eyebrows above them were bright white. His unkempt hair was the color of steel. He was wearing what McMurray recognized as business clothes, although they were very used looking, and ill-fitting. The jacket was too large, while the pants rested several inches above the man's ankles. His white socks looked brand new, as did his running shoes.

McMurray kept his eyes on the man's for many minutes – neither of them flinched. People were walking past to enter the restaurant, but no one paid either the dog or the man much mind, aside from a few backward glances. This might have been the East Side, but it was still Manhattan, where in McMurray's experience, people had a high tolerance for odd behavior. Finally, the man let down his guard and dropped the fly swatter inside his bag. Then he reached in and pulled out a hat with a feather in it, and placed it firmly on his head; tufts of wild curls escaped from under it wherever they could.

"Well, just so you understand it, this is my place," the man said. "I come here most every night for my dinner, which I earn free and clear entertaining folks with my music up and down the Museum Mile on Fifth Avenue over there. I guess you could say I sing for my supper. And I ain't gonna let no begging dog steal my audience!"

McMurray couldn't tell whether the man knew he could understand him, if he had some special knowledge about the world, or if he was not quite right in the head (a favorite phrase of one of the elderly humans McMurray kept company with in the park during the day).

"Now if you'll excuse me, I'm going inside to pick up my daily order of moo shuu."

McMurray's tongue fell out of his mouth. *This is him!* he thought with great excitement. *This is my business partner!* McMurray watched the man enter the restaurant, whereupon a waiter almost immediately handed him a take-out bag. In return, the man handed the waiter some bills, tipped his hat to him, and then walked back out onto the street, where he headed east. If he went far enough, McMurray knew, he would end up in a place called Queens. It was now quite dark. McMurray headed west, back to his side of the park.

In the morning, he returned to the East Side. He trotted up and down Fifth Avenue, as inconspicuously as he could, looking for the man he had met the night before. There were many dog walkers about, traveling with large assortments of canines. It was easy enough for McMurray to tag along, looking enough like he belonged that no one paid him any mind. Except for the other dogs, of course, who shot him strange looks more often than they actually said anything. When on occasion one did ask, "And just what do you think you're doing?" they usually got reprimanded by their dog walker for barking. McMurray found this quite amusing.

It took McMurray half the day before he found the man he was looking for, sitting on one of the many steps that led to the entrance of a big, fancy building. *This must be one of the places where the important things hang,* McMurray thought. The man was sitting toward the bottom of the lengthy, stone staircase, running his fingers across the strings of what McMurray had come to know as a guitar. Kids often played them in the park, but not as well as this man. His fingers were moving very fast, and he was singing along in a raspy voice. From what McMurray could understand of the song, someone had left the man, and he was feeling very bad about it.

The box which held the man's guitar was on the stair below him, wide open, and every now and then people threw in coins, just they did with the fountain in the park. McMurray lay down next to the box, his head resting between his two front paws. He looked up imploringly at the people who had gathered to listen to the old man, who was doing a good job of ignoring him.

When the man finished his song, he said, "Thank you ladies and gentleman. Now if you don't mind, it's intermission time." He tipped his hat to them as they dispersed, then turned his attention to McMurray.

"Now, what did I tell you last night? This is my territory. You need to scat!"

It was McMurray's turn to ignore him. He ignored him all afternoon, as he played for the crowds of people who came to visit the big building, only stopping once to buy a hot dog from a nearby vendor. He didn't share with McMurray, but that was okay. The tourists were offering him bits of their hot dogs and soft pretzels. Besides, McMurray was waiting for a bigger payoff than a dirty water hotdog. To prove he deserved it, at the end of each song he barked along with the clapping onlookers, and even stood on his hind legs and twirled a bit for their amusement.

As the afternoon waned, the crowds thinned. The old man stayed out there until sunset though. Then he emptied his guitar box, carefully straightening all the paper money and counting all the coins. When he was finished, he looked up at McMurray.

"Best day I had all week. Best day I had in a long time."

"Darn straight!" McMurray barked back.

"You know, I had a partner like you once. Helped me work the crowds. But then I had to move to a place that didn't allow no dogs, and, well…" The man's voice trailed off, then came back with a vengeance. "So you know you can't stay with me. I can't give you no home! Best I can do is share my moo shu."

McMurray barked in acceptance of the terms. The moo shu was all he wanted. Beginning that day and for several years thereafter, McMurray met this man, whom he soon learned was named Eddie, every morning at the East 72nd Street entrance to the park. Together, they performed for the patrons of the many museums that lined Fifth Avenue. And this is how McMurray got his first day job. It was something in which he took great pride – he, a mere mutt, working in partnership with a human, earning his own moo shu in Manhattan.

Over the years, McMurray became acquainted not just with the ways of humans, but with the different ways his own kind. There was an entire community of canines who, like McMurray, managed to live freely in the parks and streets of Manhattan. They existed independently of humans, but not of each other – they were an organized pack, with a leader who claimed to be part wolf.

This alpha dog went by the name Malachi. He was lean, with sharp fangs and a quick temper. His gray fur was thick and short, although it grew in fuller around his neck, giving him the appearance of having a mane, like the statues of lions McMurray saw in the city. Malachi told all dogs who crossed his path how he lost one of his eyes when he was very young, to a human child who pelted him with rocks. Malachi's pack was at least seven strong – sometimes it was greater. He picked up strays here and there, but not all of them stayed for the duration. Not all were invited to.

McMurray was familiar with the pack, but he never officially joined it; instead, he remained on the fringes, running with them when he got lonely, or bored. He remembered what he had been taught, and never overstepped his bounds. If there was food, he didn't partake unless invited. If there was space to sleep, he didn't lie down unless Malachi had given him permission. And it wasn't just for the sake of good manners, or because of his mother's warning.

McMurray saw how intimidated humans were of this pack of wild dogs when they caught glimpses of them in the park. They ran from them, and with good reason. Some of these dogs were truly vicious. They were not only a threat to humans, but McMurray had watched them tear each other apart over something as petty as squirrel meat. There were thousands of squirrels in the parks, yet these dogs were willing to rip each other's throats out over one. Most of the dogs in Malachi's pack bore the scars of battle – missing eyes, torn ears, bald patches.

When McMurray saw these dogs bare their teeth and growl at humans, a chill ran down his spine. He didn't want humans to put a harness on him, but he didn't want them to be mortally afraid of him either. McMurray knew Malachi looked down on him for how he peacefully co-existed with humans, and that he probably wouldn't have been allowed to join the pack, even if he had wanted to.

"I don't trust a dog who's so cozy with the enemy," Malachi told him.

McMurray believed that Malachi let him hang with the pack only because he wanted to keep his one good eye on him. But the group of dogs Malachi truly despised were the ones whose owners dressed them up and proudly trotted around the park. "Traitors," Malachi called this privileged set.

McMurray had to admit he couldn't identify with this group at all – dogs who actually *preferred* a domesticated life. There were many more of these dogs in the parks than the wild or stray kind, and they usually only came out during the day, always on the short end of a leash or harness. In the winter, even the big, furry ones tended to be dressed in wool coats and booties. When it rained, they donned rubber coats and rubber booties, and walked beneath the comfort of a king-size umbrella. Then there were the dogs who didn't have to walk at all; instead, these vulnerable creatures were pushed around in carriages, the same way human babies were. McMurray imagined what the pads of their paws must look like, how smooth they must be, like a pup's.

These spoiled uptown dogs were just as powerful in their tameness as the untamed dogs were in their wildness. McMurray could see that. Their humans built their lives around them. But something about it was fishy to McMurray. He wondered if there was anything dog-like about these pampered pets that had survived their humanizing, their wearing of clothes and lack of exercise. *After all, doesn't a dog first and foremost desire to be a dog?* he asked himself.

As much as he didn't like to admit it, McMurray was much more attracted to what he called the "penthouse pooches" than he was to the wild pack from the park. One penthouse pooch in particular had garnered his affection from the very first time he'd seen her out for a walk. Little did McMurray know, this poodle held the key to much more than his heart.

CHAPTER FOUR –

In Which We Meet Our Heroine, the Fabulous Miss Fifi

M<small>CMURRAY HAD BEEN ON</small> his own for about seven years the first time he laid eyes on Fifi "the Duchess of Marigold" VanCandor, although he didn't yet know her name. He'd been waiting for Eddie at East 72nd Street when he suddenly caught her scent as she walked down Fifth Avenue toward him. *Va-va-va-voom*, he thought to himself, as he took in the high-class looks of this perfectly-coiffed poodle donning a red, satin bow on each of her snow white ears. He wasn't sure what the phrase meant, but every time a well-proportioned human woman walked by, one of the old men McMurray used to sit with in the park would say, "Va-va-va-voom!" and whistle.

McMurray couldn't whistle, so he let out a soft "Grrr," being careful not to call too much attention to himself. He wanted to approach this fine canine creature, but he thought the human on the other end of the leash would disapprove. He wasn't sure what the poodle's reaction would be either. He did manage to catch her attention as she and sauntered by, entering the park closely heeled to her walker. McMurray's eyes met hers for just a moment. If she was interested in becoming more intimately acquainted, she didn't let on, but instead continued to proceed neatly down the path. Thirty seconds later, Eddie arrived, and off to work they went.

This went on every morning for the next three days. *She must be new to this neighborhood*, McMurray concluded. *I certainly would've noticed her before.*

McMurray hadn't had any great loves during his lifetime – a few flirtations here and there, but nothing to howl about. He was wary of getting attached. And although he was fascinated by them, he certainly never would've thought of trying to ingratiate himself with a penthouse pooch. They were notoriously silent and standoffish, males and females alike. *It's almost like they're keeping a secret*, McMurray thought on more than one occasion. He picked up on the knowing glances they exchanged, the slight nods of the head – and once or twice he even thought he caught them winking at each other. He had to admit, he was slightly intimidated by this group, just as he was of Malachi's pack. McMurray was the consummate outsider. Still, he could sense that there was something different about this poodle, something special that drew him to her.

On the fifth day of Fifi spotting, McMurray saw an opportunity to get up close and personal with her, and decided he couldn't live with himself if he let it pass. Her young walker had stopped to buy coffee from a street vendor near the entrance to the park; he started chatting up a female human who was doing the same. Fifi was sitting patiently a few feet away, waiting for him to finish his conversation. McMurray cautiously made his move. As quietly as possible, he walked over and crouched down under the bench next to where she was standing. He released a soft *grrr* from his throat, which went unnoticed by the nearby humans, but worked as planned with the pretty poodle.

She stretched her retractable harness a few more inches to get close enough to McMurray for them to communicate quietly. "It took you long enough," was the first thing she sounded out to him, in a throaty, yet very feminine manner.

"It's not easy to get you alone," McMurray responded defensively.

"Goodness gracious, don't worry about Wyatt. He's got a one track mind."

"Who's Wyatt?"

"Wyatt – my walker," she responded, seeming a bit agitated at his slowness.

"What's your name?" McMurray asked sheepishly, suddenly feeling very insecure.

"The papers from my breeder give me the name Duchess of Marigold. My humans call me Fifi. What about you?"

"I have no papers, and I have no humans. The name's McMurray."

Fifi smiled at him, so much as a dog can smile. It made him uncomfortable, so he kept on talking, so much as a dog can talk. "You new to this part of town?" he continued.

"No, not really," she answered. "I've lived on East 75th Street since I was eight weeks old. The walker before Wyatt liked to take me around the city – she had friends she met along the way, while they were out running their daily errands. Wyatt prefers to walk in the park. It gives him more of an opportunity to socialize."

"And what do you prefer?"

Again, Fifi smiled. "I prefer the indoors," she said, surprising McMurray.

"You must live in a pretty nice place then."

"Yes, in a penthouse, actually." Now it was McMurray's turn to smile. *A true penthouse pooch*, he said to himself. To him, an apartment, no matter how fancy, was nothing more than a prison.

"Don't knock it before you've tried it," Fifi scolded him, as if reading his mind.

"Inside is inside," McMurray growled, embarrassed that she could so easily tell what he was thinking. She ignored him.

"My human, Edith VanCandor, is the mistress of one of Manhattan's first families. She is a very important person and is connected to very important people," Fifi informed him.

"So, you get fancy food served in a fancy bowl, and don't get wet when it rains. Other than that, what does your owner's importance have to do with you?" McMurray asked, deciding that he didn't like this poodle close up as much as he did from afar.

"My owner? My *owner*? How dare you! I told you Edith was my human. I have no owner!" Fifi shot back.

Could that be? McMurray asked himself. *Could Fifi have found a way to beat the system? To live in the lap of luxury, yet still be her own dog?* He suddenly began to like her again, although he had no idea what to make of her. One thing was clear – Fifi was mad.

"And what kind of life do you lead, sir, that makes you feel you have the right to judge the rest of us, without knowing a thing about us?" she demanded.

McMurray thought a moment before responding. Fifi had a point. He had judged her and the rest of the penthouse pooches based simply on what he saw of their lives, not what he knew about them. Then again, none of them had ever chosen to speak to him prior to this. *Snobs*, he thought when they walked by, their well-coifed heads held high. But he realized that he was perhaps being just as big of a snob. And this penthouse pooch seemed to be giving him a chance. He chose to take it.

McMurray gave Fifi the abridged version of his life. He told her about his mother and the basement in which he was born with his four brothers. He told her about the flood and the shelter and his brief time with the Farbers. He explained to her how he had gotten by all those years, about his ability to navigate the city and his partnership with Eddie. As McMurray told her all this, Fifi's expression, even her rigid posture, softened.

"Well, Mr. McMurray. It seems you've led quite a life. Although some of the details sound too fantastic to be true."

"I promise they are. And please — it's just McMurray, the same as my mother called me."

"Did you ever find out what happened to your mother, McMurray? Or your brothers?" Fifi asked.

"No, I haven't seen any of them. Sometimes I see a dog from a distance, and I think maybe he looks like one of my brothers... but it never is," McMurray admitted. "To tell true, I try not to think about them at all."

"Well, why not? Is it too painful?"

McMurray felt he had already let his guard down too much with Fifi. After all, they had just met. He certainly didn't want her getting the wrong idea about his prowess. He was tough. He was a *dog's* dog.

"Of course not!" he shot back. "It's just that, what am I gonna do about it? The situation is out of my paws."

"Oh, my dear, McMurray! I'm sure there's a thing or two you could teach me, but that's nothing compared to what I can teach you about how things really work around here." Then Fifi's voice got very soft. "Manhattan," she whispered quietly, "bows at our paws."

"Hey, Fifi! What are you doing over there?"

Wyatt and the young woman had finished their conversation, and he turned his attention back to his job. Fifi ignored him. "Meet me here tomorrow!" she barked at McMurray, who was staring at her, astonished by what he had just heard.

At that moment, Eddie appeared. "Hey, dog! Don't get lazy on me now. The day's just startin'! Get up off the ground there and let's get to work." Eddie had been considerate enough not to bestow yet another name on McMurray which wasn't really his — he referred to him as "dog" and McMurray liked it just fine.

See, I wasn't making things up, McMurray thought as he

listened to Eddie chide him. Fifi smiled, again seeming to read his mind.

McMurray, in a show of good manners, let Fifi be the first to walk away. He watched as she and Wyatt sauntered off together toward the park. When they were out of sight, he crawled out from under the bench.

"That your girlfriend?" Eddie teased. "Fine looking poodle, that's for sure. You don't think she's a little much for you to take on, though? A dog like that isn't gonna be happy livin' on moo shu pork."

McMurray wasn't sure of anything. He hadn't responded when Fifi told him to meet her there the next day. He hadn't made any promises he needed to keep. If he didn't know his hearing was so immaculate, he would've thought he misheard the comment she made about humans bowing to dogs. *How is that possible?* he asked himself. Maybe she was the one who was lying, who wasn't quite right in the head. Besides, he had a good thing going with Eddie – why should he risk messing that up? Maybe Fifi was making a joke, or laying a trap of some kind. What reason did he have to trust her?

All of these thoughts were running through his head as he walked up Fifth Avenue, with Eddie humming at his side. For the rest of the day, McMurray tried desperately to put Miss Fifi "the Duchess of Marigold" VanCandor out of his mind. By the time the sun set, he had decided he was not going to meet her the next morning. Listening to Eddie sing about his problems with women all day helped him make up his mind. "Fifi's nothin' but trouble," he told himself.

He got his moo shu, and went back to the park to find a comfortable place to curl up. He was surprised at how easily sleep came, at how successful he'd been at clearing his head of what happened that morning. Then again, he always did have a knack for moving on. He would have moved on too, if he hadn't awoken to discover that overnight his world had been turned upside down. And that perhaps he wasn't the dog he thought he was.

CHAPTER FIVE –

Our Tale Unfolds

A ND NOW, DEAR HUMAN, you are well-informed of the life and times of our hero. You have been introduced to our heroine. Now, the story can truly begin. For this is not simply a biography of one of the finest canines ever known to dog-kind. This is not only an exposé on the true rulers of the city. It is also a mystery. And a love story. It is, in fact, a story about many different kinds of love. So let's get to it, shall we? As always, the best place to begin is at the beginning. So, without further ado, allow me take you back there.

McMurray stretched his sturdy limbs and let out a contented half-sigh, half-growl. Oh, but the sun felt *so* good. He lay drowsily on the ground, basking in the heat of the sunlit sidewalk. Although he preferred to rest on his side, he soon rolled onto his back so as to allow the warm, morning breeze to tickle his ample belly hairs. Then, as he always did after a good rest, he extended his four legs and turned over until he was standing on them, and shook out his full, reddish-brown coat of hair.

"Now, *that* was a nice little catnap," McMurray chuckled to himself.

It was more than a catnap; it was one of the best nights of sleep McMurray had had in a long while. He was proud of himself for working up the courage to approach Fifi, and even prouder that he knew when to leave well enough alone. He had been told that curiosity was a feline fault, and he was inclined to believe it. While McMurray was open to taking risks in his youth – his escape from the Farbers chief among them – he was more careful in his middle age. By his count of the seasons, he knew he was roughly eight in human years. *Too old*, he told himself, *not to know better. Too old to mess with a good thing.*

That good thing was his partnership with Eddie, which allowed him both the security of knowing where his next meal was coming from and his freedom. All of the people who stopped to take in their performances assumed that the clever dog with the handsome, red coat went home with the aging blues singer when the sun went down. Although entertained by them, no one cared enough about either the dog or the old man to make sure they had a home to which to go. McMurray was fine with that – it served his purpose. But he had a feeling, based on the content of Eddie's songs, that his partner wouldn't have minded some human companionship. The word "lonely" came up a lot.

The night before, McMurray and Eddie had parted in their customary way. Eddie gave him his supper, which included a generous portion of barbecue spare ribs, and then said, as he always did, "Now scat, dog. Ain't nothin' more for you here. Maybe I'll see you tomorrow, maybe I won't. But I do thank you for today." And then he'd tip his hat and shuffle off toward the subway.

McMurray assumed that when Eddie said, "Maybe I'll see you tomorrow, maybe I won't," he was thinking that Animal

Control might intervene, or McMurray would wander off somewhere, as dogs were known to do. It never occurred to him that Eddie might be the one who disappeared. Yet that morning, the morning after McMurray's best night of sleep in a long while, he found himself waiting for a partner who never showed.

McMurray wandered along Fifth Avenue by himself, to the steps of the big building, to see if Eddie had decided to perform without him. But he wasn't there. This went on for five days, and each night McMurray's sleep grew to be less and less. It wasn't just the grumbling of his unsatisfied tummy that was keeping him up – he had survived on scraps before. No, there was a feeling gnawing at him that had nothing to do with hunger. The last time he'd experienced it was when he went back to the Chumpskis' house and realized that his separation from his mother and siblings was more than likely permanent. McMurray could understand feeling bad about losing his family. But feeling bad about losing a human was something new to him, and it went against everything he believed in. Still, when he recalled the words Eddie moaned as he strummed his guitar, about how his baby went away and left him all alone, McMurray couldn't help but whimper.

"He was good to me," McMurray thought, defending his emotions. "He didn't give me a name that wasn't mine. He just called me dog."

And now, without explanation, he was gone. And so was McMurray's security.

McMurray still kept an eye out for Eddie, but not wanting to "play the fool," as Eddie used to sing, he primarily focused on finding a new partner. The nights were growing longer and colder, which McMurray knew meant soon the leaves would fall from the trees and icy flakes would fall from the sky – and there would be less people wandering around the city to take money from. If he was going to seal a new deal, he had to do it soon.

McMurray set his sights on teaming up with another performer; he felt he had the most to contribute to that line of work, with his dancing and tricks. He located a young woman in the park who played the guitar, like Eddie, and didn't shoo him away, as so many others had. Instead, she let him stay by her side all day. He listened politely, his pointy ears cocked, while she sang in a pitch McMurray found too high to be soothing, about some of the same things Eddie did, except now it was the men who were doing wrong. She used the word "love" a lot – apparently no one was going to love the men that left her better than she could. It made little sense to McMurray why anyone would want to, in light of all the lying and cheating they did.

McMurray noticed that, despite what was being said about them, it was mostly men who stopped to listen for a song or two, usually while munching on a hot dog they'd just bought from the cart that was stationed nearby. In between songs, McMurray would entertain the small crowd in whatever way he thought would please them most – howling along with the applause, twirling on his hind legs. He even managed a back flip, doing his utmost to impress his potential new partner who seemed to be doing quite well for herself. In exchange for money, she allowed people to take what she called her "CD." By the time the sun was on its way down, she had very few left in the box, and a lot of green bills in their place.

As the young woman gathered her belongings, McMurray sat and waited patiently for his share of the take. All he'd eaten that day was a piece of hot dog a small human had accidentally dropped on the ground. His partner hadn't eaten much either – mostly orange colored sticks she'd pulled from inside her bag which didn't look at all appetizing so he forgave her for not sharing. Packed up for the day, guitar case in hand, the young woman bent down in front of McMurray; her long, yellow hair fell in his face, tickling his nose. He held out his paw expectantly.

"What's the matter, boy?" she asked him. "Don't you have a home?"

McMurray liked how her hair smelled sweet, like the strawberry ice cream small humans sometimes let him lick from their cones, before their mothers screamed at them not to. He really was hungry. *This could be the start of something good,* he thought. But the day's events soon took an unanticipated turn.

"Officer, excuse me, officer! Sir? I think this dog over here's a stray!" the young woman shouted as she waved her hand, trying to catch the attention of a man dressed in blue who was talking to the hot dog vendor.

"Seriously?" McMurray barked at her. "You weren't so concerned about my situation when I was helping you make all that dough! Geesh! What's a dog gotta do to catch a break around here?"

Realizing he wasn't doing himself any favors by sticking around to give the young woman a piece of his mind, McMurray quickly turned and made a run for it. He headed up Fifth Avenue, staying close to the stone wall that bordered the park, the shadow of which provided him some protection from the sight of humans. Then he smelled it – the distinct scent of water about to fall from the sky. Usually he was prepared, was able to seek shelter in time. But that day he'd been paying more attention to the young woman than anything else, trying so hard to impress her. He missed the gathering rain clouds which were now emptying their cold contents on him so quickly that he was drenched inside the span of a minute.

Where'd my hard work get me? he asked himself. *Soaking wet and starving, running from the men in blue.*

It was then that he saw her. She was across the street, under the shelter of a very large, orange umbrella that was impossible to miss, even in the near dark. She was wearing a pink coat and her ears were adorned with matching pink ribbons. The rain that was falling in his eyes blurred his vision a bit, but there was no doubt in McMurray's mind that he was gazing at his favorite penthouse pooch, the fabulous Miss Fifi. He watched as a man – not Wyatt the walker this time, but someone older and better fed – scooped her up with the hand that wasn't holding the umbrella.

"Poor princess can't get her precious paws wet," McMurray barked, apparently louder than he'd intended for both the man and Miss Fifi turned their heads in his direction. Instead of running, McMurray took the opportunity to show the pampered poodle how a real dog managed in the rain. He took a few steps forward and sat down, remaining perfectly still as the water pelted his fur.

In the face of McMurray's show of toughness, Fifi remained silent. She in fact turned her well-coifed head away from him, which seemed to signal to the man gingerly cradling her was that it was time to go.

I guess I earned that, McMurray admitted to himself. *I did blow her off.*

He watched as the poodle and her person, whoever he was, started to walk further uptown. McMurray looked around. The sidewalks were emptying themselves of humans as the rain continued to pour down. In their rush to get inside a yellow car, or inside a building, the people were paying him no mind. At that moment he knew he was feeling what Eddie spent so much time singing about – lonely. Not knowing where else to go or what else to do, McMurray lifted his hind quarters off the cold cement and started following Fifi and her human, who were presumably heading home.

It wasn't far, just a few blocks. The building was what McMurray had expected – big and fancy. There was no front stoop, like so many buildings on the other side of town had. Instead, there was a red and gold awning that marked the entrance. The door was made of glass, and was surrounded by big windows that afforded McMurray a good look inside. A man wearing a hat similar in shape to the ones the men in blue wore and a brown jacket came out to hold the door open for Fifi and her person; he tipped his hat to them, the same way Eddie had tipped his hat to him every night. McMurray watched from what he considered a safe distance as Fifi's person placed her on the dry ground inside. The room they were in was dimly lit; still, McMurray could see that there were several sparkling jars full of fresh flowers. The man in the hat walked over to the wall and pushed a button, and moments later a sliding door opened and Fifi's person followed her into it. The door slid shut and they were gone. The man in the hat went and stood behind a desk, staring out the glass door at the rain. It appeared to McMurray that the man was staring straight at him; if he was, he didn't give any indication that he saw him.

A long, black car pulled up directly in front of the entrance, forcing McMurray to change his vantage point so he could see the man in the hat come through the door once again. This time he had an open umbrella with which to shield the person he was helping exit the car. A gloved hand accepted the man's extended arm, and a body draped in the fur of some unfortunate animal followed. In the winter, McMurray saw many women wearing coats like this; although he knew the coats weren't made of dogs' fur, the sight always caused him to shudder. On this occasion, he was also shivering from the cold.

If I were a betting dog I'd venture being cold and wet isn't something this lady knows too much about, he thought as he watched the man in the hat lead what was clearly an older woman inside Fifi's building. McMurray watched as the woman disappeared into the sliding door the same way Fifi and her person had. The long, black car drove away, and McMurray saw the man in the hat assume his post behind the desk once more.

The sky was now very dark, and the rain showed no sign of relenting. McMurray looked up at the building which housed Fifi; he knew she lived in the penthouse, but the building seemed to go on forever and he couldn't make out any top floor windows from his spot on the ground below. He imagined how dry and warm she must be all the way up there.

The one and only time they'd spoken, Fifi told him what seemed to be a well-guarded secret: "Manhattan bows at our paws." It was certainly news to him. McMurray hadn't given anything she said much credibility, but now that he had a glimpse of her world, a world so different from anything he'd ever known even during his time living with humans, he had to admit he was curious.

"Just because curiosity does cats in, that doesn't mean sniffing around a little is gonna get the best of me," McMurray reassured himself with a low growl. "I'm tough! I'm a dog's dog!" he barked. Then he began sneezing uncontrollably – our hero was coming down with a cold.

"Tomorrow," he whimpered. "I'll get to the bottom of things tomorrow."

Under the cover of a rainy, night sky that had effectively cleared the sidewalks of humans, McMurray made his way back to the park to the sound of many honking horns; he had no problem safely crossing streets, as whenever it rained or snowed the traffic in the city came to a near standstill. He had long marveled at how humans cared more about staying dry than they did about getting where they're going. Where McMurray was going that night he hadn't a clue; Malachi's pack secured the park's driest hide-outs, and when he took up with Eddie, McMurray forfeited even his limited acceptance with that gang.

McMurray found a man sleeping on a bench; he'd covered himself with newspaper, which had done precious little to keep him dry. McMurray curled up under the bench, using the man's body as protection from the raindrops. He didn't have the energy to forage for food that evening, and he was so exhausted, his hunger didn't prevent him falling into a fast, albeit fitful, sleep.

That night McMurray dreamed of things he'd done his best

to put out of his mind – his days in the Chumpskis' basement, evenings spent running through the park with his mother and siblings, his return to the Chumpskis' which instead of offering him hope, forced him to accept that he'd never see his family again. When he woke the next morning, he was just as tired as when he laid his head down the evening before. The man on the bench was gone; only the soggy newspapers gave a hint that he was ever there. McMurray was famished, and still a little wet. The rain was gone, but the sky was gray, signaling the beginning of a new, less friendly season.

McMurray stood and shook the dampness out of his knotted fur. He shivered in spite of himself; he hated when his body betrayed any sign of weakness. He knew that birds flew south, to warmer places, for the winter, and that humans sometimes did the same. *Perhaps I'm getting too old for this*, he thought. *Perhaps there is a better way.*

With that idea foremost in his mind, he set out to find Miss Fifi.

CHAPTER SIX –

To Forgive is Human?

M cMurray knew his chance of finding leftovers he'd actually want to eat after a heavy rainstorm like the one the city had just experienced was slim. Any garbage he could easily get to would be thoroughly soaked. He decided it was best to get down to business, and wait until later to answer the groans of his aching belly.

McMurray's belly wasn't the only thing aching. His head was throbbing and every now and then a sneeze would escape his tender nose. His sturdy legs felt a little wobbly beneath him as he made his way back to the building that he saw Fifi enter with her person the evening before. She wouldn't be leaving for her morning walk for some time; McMurray's plan was to catch her as she set out and walk along with her, so they would have time to talk. She being a female and he being a male – and given what he'd learned about women from Eddie – McMurray figured that he'd be doing some begging of a different order when he came into contact with Fifi.

"They like to see us on our knees, our sweethearts do," Eddie once explained to him about a song he'd just finished singing. "Just like the rest of the world."

McMurray wasn't sure that dogs ever got down on their knees, whatever those were, but he'd learned a thing or two about begging during his years on the streets. He had an "only when necessary" rule that applied the act; he had a feeling that in order to get Fifi to speak to him again, it was going to be necessary.

He curled up underneath a mailbox across the street from her home and waited for her to appear. There was a different man standing inside at the desk than the one who'd been there the night before, but he was dressed exactly the same. This one had hair on his face though, just above his lip, and the sleeves of his brown jacket were too long, mostly covering his hands which he kept stiffly at his sides.

The door that Fifi, her person, and the woman in fur disappeared into the night before slid open and this time, out walked a group of five dogs; McMurray was relieved to see Fifi among them, wearing the same red ribbons as the first time they met. He recognized Wyatt the walker, pulling up the rear. When he'd seen Fifi previously she'd been alone, and he was counting on the fact that Wyatt was easily distracted in order to get some quality time with her. But this worked out better; McMurray could blend into the group, assuming it was a friendly one. He crossed the street and hid behind a potted plant next to the building's entrance.

The man in the cap opened the door and Wyatt, still trailing behind, shouted out, "Thanks, bro!" which seemed odd since McMurray was fairly certain the man opened the door for the dogs and not for him.

Once outside, Wyatt positioned himself in front of the group; instead of heading towards the park, Wyatt turned left and led the dogs east. *Maybe this is why it's been so easy to avoid her,* McMurray thought. *She hasn't been going to the park. Maybe she won't be able to pin our not meeting again on me.*

With a renewed sense of confidence, McMurray joined the back of the privileged pack. Fifi was up ahead, walking next to another poodle who looked very much like her, but was distinctly male. Behind them were two Pomeranians. And pulling up the rear with McMurray was a Burmese Mountain Dog, the large size of which made McMurray's presence fairly unremarkable – except to the Burmese Mountain Dog.

"And just what do you think you're doing? This isn't a charity walk," the Burmese growled at him.

"It's a free country. I have every much a right to be on this sidewalk as you do," McMurray shot back, echoing a sentiment he'd heard many times from the men who slept on benches at the park.

"Suit yourself," his large walking partner replied, "I was raised in a libertarian household. But stay downwind of me, please. You need a bath – with soap."

"What's going on back there?" the Pomeranians barked simultaneously.

"We have a freeloader in our midst, friends. Never fear. Despite the way he smells, he appears to be quite harmless."

"Forget you!" McMurray barked at the Burmese. "I thought you fancy guys were supposed to have manners!"

"Good manners, my dear sir, include not going where one hasn't been invited."

"*Good manners, my dear sir, include not going where one hasn't been invited,*" McMurray mimicked in a high-pitched yelp. "Could you be any less of a real dog?"

"Oh no he didn't!" the Pomeranians gasped in unison.

"He most certainly did," the Burmese barked. "In defense of my honor, I must challenge you to a duel, sir. Fernando will stand in as my second!"

"A duel? What's a duel? And who's Fernando?" McMurray barked back.

The Burmese stopped in his large tracks. "A duel is something I saw on television, on the History Channel. It's what humans do when one offends another."

"See, right there. That's just what I mean. What *humans* do. Do you have any idea what dogs do?"

"In a situation such as this? How would I? I've never been subjected to such uncouth behavior before from one of my own, if I can dare call you that."

"Un*what* behavior?"

"Uncouth. It means rude. You are a rude, red beast!"

All of the barking – and the fact that his charges had stopped moving – finally caught Wyatt's attention.

"What the heck is going on back there?" he shouted. "Bobo, did you make a new friend, boy?"

"Bobo? *Bobo?*" McMurray cackled. "I'm trading barbs with a dog named Bobo?"

"My humans let the children name me. It's endearing, really. And as Shakespeare wrote, *what's in a name?* I happen to think I carry it quite well."

"You just go on thinking that, buddy. Whatever gets you through the night." Despite his mockery of Bobo, McMurray couldn't help but feel a twinge of sympathy; after all, the Farbers had let their child name him Barkley.

"What gets me through the night is sleeping on 600 thread count Egyptian cotton," was Bobo's retort.

"Listen, there's no need to talk so much, bub. I got no clue about most of what you're saying," McMurray told him.

"Not surprising."

"Well, you boys seem to be getting along okay," Wyatt interrupted. "And the more the merrier, right? Oh, but red dude, there's a leash law. You can't hang with us if you're not on a leash. I can't risk losing this gig."

McMurray saw that Fifi was sitting at Wyatt's side, trying very hard to ignore him. He wondered if that poodle she was with was her mate. The thought of facing that humiliation almost made him turn tail, but knowing that he'd never get another chance, now that he'd called so much attention to himself, he chose to subject himself to a larger humiliation.

McMurray walked over to Wyatt and sat obediently at his feet. He let his tongue hang loose and forced as much of a smile as he could. He was hungry, he was tired – and he wanted answers. As much as it pained him to admit it, he had a feeling that this group had them. He bowed his head, hoping that Wyatt, as thick as he was, would understand the signal.

"So, you wanna hang with us, huh? All right then." McMurray watched as Wyatt took out of his backpack that thing which McMurray had run from when he fled the Farbers' Volvo; that thing which he had been running from almost as long as he could remember. In Wyatt's hand was quite possibly the end of McMurray's life as he knew it, but it might also represent the beginning of a new and improved life. Only time would tell.

"I don't have a harness, just this choke chain. Just don't pull and it won't hurt you," Wyatt warned as he bent down and slipped the metal collar over McMurray's neck. McMurray was panting in anticipation of the moment when he felt the collar squeeze around him, cutting off his air. To his surprise, he was still able to breathe quite normally.

"Remember, don't pull!" Wyatt told him again. McMurray barked to let him know he understood. "You're a good boy," Wyatt said, patting him on the head. "We'll have to see what we can do about finding you a home."

At hearing that, McMurray dug his hind feet into the ground. Wyatt, who had started walking, stopped short, and McMurray felt the collar close tightly around his neck. *What have I done?* he thought, beginning to panic. *I have no idea where he's taking me, and now I'm trapped!"* McMurray cried out involuntarily.

"Oh, come on now, boy. I didn't mean to hurt you. It'll be okay. Just walk when I walk."

"Listen to him, McMurray. It really will be okay," Fifi said in a softer tone than he'd expected given the way she'd been glaring at him only moments before.

McMurray was embarrassed by his display of fear, but glad that the silence between them had been broken. "Can we move this along, please? I have a massage appointment at ten," Bobo barked. "It just does wonders for the pain in my hips."

"Do you know this mutt?" the male poodle chimed in.

"Yes, Fernando, as a matter of fact I do."

"Oh, yes? From where?"

"Bobo is right, Fernando – it's time to go," Fifi replied, avoiding the question.

Fifi took the lead and the rest of the dogs – and Wyatt – followed. Soon, Wyatt was trailing behind the group again. McMurray looked back and saw that he had put what he recognized to be headphones in his ears; all the runners in the park wore them. Eddie often complained that that was a lousy way to get music, when so much live talent was available.

"There's music everywhere," Eddie would say. "Just close your eyes and listen, dog. Listen to the wind blowin' through the trees. The children laughin'. Even the horns honkin'. It's all music. 'Cept these folks here ain't never gonna hear any of it. Lost in their own world, tryin' to drown out everything that means somethin'."

McMurray liked the way Eddie thought; he learned to hear the music too. But he was also glad Wyatt wasn't able to hear the barking that ensued after he put his headphones on. He and Fifi had a lot to talk about, and her friends weren't exactly the types to mind their own business.

"Long time no see," McMurray said to Fifi, trying to sound as casual as possible.

"And whose fault is that?"

"Well, you've been taking this new route and all…"

"Don't you even try it!" she barked at him, sounding rather vicious. "I chose this new route after you stood me up by the park. Two mornings I waited for you. I told myself that you didn't deserve a second chance, after you didn't show the first morning. But I convinced myself to give you one. And what did I get for my efforts, for putting myself out there like that? Not a darn thing. Do you have any idea how that feels?"

"Well, actually, just yesterday…"

"And another thing! Bobo was right. You do need a bath – with soap."

"Geez, I'm really sorry, Fifi." McMurray hung his tail between his legs in a show of genuine repentance.

"What's the matter, Fi? Do you need me to step in and take care of this tough guy for you?"

"Oh please, Fernando," Fifi yapped. "I'd like to see you try."

"Is this guy *your* guy?" McMurray asked.

"Goodness, no! Fernando is my brother. Don't you see the resemblance?"

"Yes, but…"

"His human and my human are friends. They got us from the same breeder, the same litter. We don't live together though. We are only dogs."

"Okay. And the rest of these guys – who are they? They don't appear to be more of your relatives."

"No. We all live in the same building though. Fernando lives in penthouse number two. The Epstein twins – the Pomeranians behind us – reside on the eighth floor. And Bobo – you've met Bobo. Bobo lives on the eleventh."

"The last time I saw you, you weren't all walking together like this."

"Edith, my human – remember I told you about her? Edith is trying to help Wyatt cultivate more business. She loves to support young talent, and believe it or not, Wyatt is a classical pianist attending Juliard."

"I believe it. I have no idea what Juliard is."

"Oh, McMurray. It's a school here in Manhattan where the most gifted humans come to study the arts."

"Oh, I see," McMurray responded, although he really didn't.

"Edith met Wyatt one evening at a cocktail party. He'd

been hired to play the piano. He explained that he was a musician paying his own way through school and that he also had a dog walking business on the side. And that is how Wyatt came into my life. Now Edith is trying to get other humans in the building to hire him."

McMurray waited for Fifi to continue; she'd barely stopped talking since she started. After a few moments, he decided it would be all right for him to say something. He chose his words carefully, not wanting to say anything that would upset her.

"I've noticed there are lots of people in the city who play music. I used to have a gig with one of them."

"Yes, I remember you told me about your friend. What was his name? Eddie? Why aren't you with him now?"

"He disappeared. I haven't seen him for almost a week – not since the day I met you. That was the last day Eddie and I worked together."

"Is that why you stood me up?"

"Listen, I didn't stand you up. We never had a real date. I mean, you asked me to meet you, but I never said I would."

"Well, if you don't desire my company, what are you doing here now then?" Fifi barked, clearly wounded by what McMurray had just said to her.

"Yes, please do tell why you have graced us with your pungent presence, dear boy," Bobo joined in.

"I've just...I've had a rough time of it these last few days. And I remember you said something about how the humans..."

Fifi began to bark furiously, seemingly at a snooty Chihuahua that was being wheeled by in a baby carriage.

"What did you tell him about the humans?" the Epstein twins asked.

"Yes, Fi. Do tell what you've told," Bobo said accusingly.

Fifi stopped barking. "I told him that we don't have it so bad, living with humans. Even if it means having to wear a harness. That's all."

"That's all?" Fernando demanded.

"Yes, Nando, that's all. McMurray here has been a stray most of his life. He looks down on us for our relationship with humans. I simply told him that he shouldn't judge it until he's really tried it."

"If you say so. But McMurray here looks like more of a Brooklyn bow-wow than a penthouse pooch," Fernando said, appearing to relax a bit.

"Don't be a snob, Nando."

"Don't be a bleeding heart, Fi."

"I wish all of you would just be quiet so I could enjoy my walk. I wouldn't want Wyatt here to get a bad review," Bobo said, putting an end to the conversation.

"How would he give Wyatt a bad review?" McMurray whispered.

"Use your imagination," Fifi said. "There's something very specific we're supposed to be doing out here."

"So you mean if Bobo doesn't…that he'll…*inside?*"

"Yes."

"That's awful! And he called me uncouth?"

"Until humans learn to speak canine, our means of communication are limited. It's easier with some than with others. Take Wyatt here – he seems to be able to read us quite well, and has no authority issues whatsoever. All I had to do was pull him in a different direction one day, and suddenly, my walk had a new route. Edith is like that too. She can't understand me when I speak to her, but she listens in other ways."

"Eddie was like that."

"Do you miss Eddie, McMurray?"

"I still hear talking!" Bobo reprimanded.

"Never mind. We'll talk more later, when we're home."

"But Fifi, I…"

"Shhh, McMurray!" she growled, making it clear that for now, the conversation was over.

And about 15 minutes later, so was the walk. They were

back in front of Fifi's building, and McMurray was still wearing a leash. There was no way he could make a break for it without strangling himself. So he followed Wyatt and the dogs inside, where he caught a glimpse of himself in the mirrored walls. His coat was matted and very dirty underneath by his belly. His paws were outright filthy. His eyes were runny. He could not deny that he was at that moment a messy mutt, and that Bobo was probably right about the way he smelled.

"Don't worry, McMurray. We'll get you cleaned up once we're upstairs," Fifi assured him.

"Wait. What? Upstairs?"

"So, Fifi. Do you think Mrs. VanCandor would like to help your friend, Red, out?"

Fifi let out a jubilant bark in response to Wyatt's question, and twirled around on her back paws.

"Me too. Let's drop these guys off and then introduce the two of them."

McMurray, not having much choice, followed the group through the sliding door when it opened, and proceeded to stare in awe at the tiny room, which like the larger one they'd just exited was also covered in mirrors.

"It's called an elevator," Fifi whispered, sensing McMurray's confusion. McMurray rode the elevator to the eighth floor, and then the eleventh; each time, the door opened directly into the dogs' home. Still, McMurray wasn't able to get a good view inside, his peak at how the other half lived. They had to go all the way back down to the ground floor to get a special elevator that took them to Fifi's penthouse. When the doors opened there, a man McMurray recognized was waiting.

"Our butler," Fifi explained. "You saw him out with me in the rain last night."

"And who is this?" the butler asked upon seeing McMurray.

"Not sure," Wyatt answered, removing the choke collar from around McMurray's neck. "I've been calling him Red. Fi seems to have taken a liking to him. I think he's a stray. I was hoping Mrs. VanCandor would be willing to help him out."

"Yes, well, we know how Mrs. VanCandor likes to help strays," the butler responded in a tone McMurray didn't interpret as being at all friendly. Fifi let out a low growl to show her disapproval.

"Okay, great then. I have to get Ferdinand here home now..."

"It's Fernando," the butler corrected him, again not sounding very nice.

"Yeah, right, Fernando. Sorry about that little guy," Wyatt said, rubbing the poodle behind his ears. "Anyway, let's get you home."

McMurray could sense that the butler made Wyatt very nervous. He glanced over at Fifi, who just rolled her eyes in response. After the elevator door closed, the butler turned his attention to the two of them.

"Well, I certainly can't let you roam around Mrs. VanCandor's home in this condition. Come – to the kitchen!"

Fifi followed the butler, and McMurray followed Fifi. He understood why the butler didn't want him near anything; almost everything in the home was white, from the furniture to the walls to the carpeting to the drapery.

"Edith just had it redecorated," Fifi let him know. "Before that, everything was red, and before that, yellow."

The butler led them to a small room in the back of the kitchen. "I think the laundry room is an appropriate place for you to wait. Fifi, are you coming with me?"

Fifi barked and set her haunches squarely on the heated linoleum floor, letting him know that she would in fact be staying put.

"All right then. Have it your way. I'll ring the bell when Mrs. VanCandor arrives home from her hair appointment."

The butler left the two of them there – *Finally, we're alone,* McMurray thought. *Now I can ask the important questions.* He breathed in deeply. The small room smelled nice, like flowers. Like the first day of spring. The warm floor felt so good beneath his feet. Without being able to help it, McMurray lay down and rested his head on the tile.

"That was Lars," Fifi said. "He's Edith's watchdog."

"But he's a human."

"I was speaking, what is it called...metaphorically? He's so protective of her. That's why he's so rude to Wyatt. He thinks everyone has their hand out for a piece of Edith's fortune. She is very generous."

"What do you think she's going to make of me?"

"Don't worry about that, McMurray. Why don't you just rest for now?"

"Who me? I'm not in the least bit tired."

"I'm sure you're not."

"Fifi?"

"Yes?"

"I don't know what's gonna happen here, but I want you to know, I appreciate you forgiving me for standing you up."

"But I thought you didn't stand me up?"

Fifi got no response to her question, for McMurray had already descended into a deep, dreamless sleep.

CHAPTER SEVEN –

Mrs. VanCandor, Take a Bow Wow Wow!

WHEN MCMURRAY WOKE FROM his nap, he found himself in the shadow of an unfamiliar woman who had something very familiar wrapped around her ample body – the fur McMurray spotted when he was spying on Fifi the night before. Immediately, he disliked this woman, and he would have growled at her to let her know it, if it were not for the fact that she was holding a triumphant looking Fifi close to her chest.

"Well, he certainly does need a bath, doesn't he, Lars?"

"Yes, madam."

"Did Wyatt tell you where he found him?"

"No, madam. He said that Miss Fifi had taken a liking to him. I assume they picked him up somewhere along their walk." Fifi barked in agreement. "I hope you don't mind that I let a strange dog into the house. I figured, knowing your good and generous nature, that you would want to help, er, Red."

"Not at all, Lars. Not at all. My Fifi has excellent instincts – when it comes to two- and four-legged creatures alike. If she approves of this canine...what did you call him? Red?"

"Yes, madam."

"If she approves of Red, well, than, we should try to do right by him."

"Very well, madam. Does doing right by him begin with bathing him?"

McMurray's inclination was to bolt. He remembered the baths Mrs. Farber gave him, how unpleasant they were. Although he knew he was in need of a good cleaning, he didn't understand why a jump in the Central Park Reservoir wouldn't do.

"Yes, but not here."

"Oh, heavens no, madam."

"Call the service. Tell them to bring the van around."

McMurray's ears perked up. This did not go unnoticed by Fifi. She let out a low, slow growl to help him understand that he should do what he's told. McMurray lay down and put his head between his paws; his submissive pose let Fifi know he'd heard her.

While they waited for the van to arrive, Mrs. VanCandor, who had since removed her fur, prepared a meal of boiled chicken and rice for McMurray, which she served to him in a delicate glass bowl. The meal was rather bland for McMurray's taste – after all, he was used to spicy Chinese – but he was grateful for it. He could have devoured it in under a minute, except he wanted to show Fifi that contrary to Bobo's impression of him, he was not uncouth. Still, he finished the food quickly enough to elicit a response from Mrs. VanCandor.

"Poor thing. He must have been famished," she said to Fifi as she cleared the bowl away. "We're having filet mignon for dinner tonight. Some red meat should put the pep back in his step."

McMurray began salivating at the mention of filet mignon. Unfortunately, he had to get through the business of being bathed first. Fifi's harnesses didn't fit him, so it was back to the choke collar and chain that Wyatt had so thoughtfully left behind. Lars led him downstairs in the elevator and out the front of the building, where there was, as promised, a van waiting. McMurray's mind flashed back to his trip to the animal shelter, but it didn't appear as if they were going to put him in a cage this time. Following Fifi's orders, he agreeably hopped into the van's open back doors, where he was met with an array of devices he'd never seen before.

Over the course of the next 45 minutes, he was washed, dried, snipped and clipped. And to his surprise, he enjoyed it, or at least most of it. The soap used by the two women who tended to him smelled similar to Mrs. VanCandor's laundry room – like fragrant spring flowers. Although they had to brush him aggressively to do so, it felt good to get the knots out of his hair. He could've done without getting his nails cut, but once they were, he appreciated how much easier it was to stand on his carefully and evenly pruned paws.

He had been hoping throughout the ordeal (which wasn't much of an ordeal at all), that the two women would not finish him off by putting a bow anywhere on or near him. When he saw them pull out a white bandana he was none too pleased, but decided to count his blessings as they tied it – instead of a bow – around his neck, before placing the choke collar back on and leading him out of the van. They signaled to the man inside at the desk and a few minutes later, Lars was down to retrieve him.

"Just put it on Mrs. VanCandor's account," Lars told them. "He looks just marvelous. Like a completely different dog. I'm sure Mrs. VanCandor will tip you handsomely when she pays her bill at the end of the month."

Lars led McMurray inside, where he caught the first glimpse of his much cleaner self in the mirrors that lined the walls. He did look like a completely different dog, but in a good way. The grooming had taken years off his appearance; his coat was shinier than ever, his eyes brighter. While he had been a frequent admirer of his reflection in the past, he never realized he could look this…well… *civilized* was the only word he could think of to describe it, and he was ashamed of himself for it. He had devoted his life to being *uncivilized*, and here he was, in the entrance to a penthouse building, appreciating in himself the very quality he had been running from for so long. And he knew why.

"I'll always be a mutt," he said to himself. "But now I feel like I can compete with the best of them. I feel…powerful."

That feeling only intensified as he sat next to Fifi in her immaculate white kitchen that evening (Fifi insisted that McMurray refer to everything as "hers" as opposed to "her owner's"), feasting on rare filet mignon. He was surprised, given Fifi's stature in the home, that they weren't dining with Mrs. VanCandor.

"We are not humans, McMurray. We are their companions and they ours. But it's important that a dog always remain a dog. I hope you're discovering that there's more than one way to do that – and that your way is not necessarily the right way."

"This tasty piece of meat is certainly helping me be more open minded. Does Lars eat with Edith every night? Isn't it important that a butler always remain a butler?"

"Lars has been with Edith much longer than I have – for 18 years, since her husband died. Edith married a much older man. She tells me all the time that he was the love of her life. The children from his first marriage never liked Edith very much, and they liked her even less when their father left her all of his money. Edith has been alone ever since – with her causes, her animals, and Lars."

"Animals?" McMurray inquired, as he gobbled down another piece of succulent meat.

"There's a cat, Macy, who takes all of her meals in Edith's room. Macy is old and not very sociable. Mr. VanCandor gave her to Edith just before he died. And there's a bird, Topaz, who has free reign of the sun porch, which used to be the terrace before Edith enclosed it. But I think we need to talk more about what you said about Lars," Fifi said, stepping away from her food.

"What? What did I say? Are you going to finish that?"

"No, help yourself, please. You said something about a butler knowing his place."

"I don't think that's what I said," McMurray responded, while finishing off Fifi's filet.

"Well, in a roundabout way you did. You see, Edith didn't always have money. She doesn't believe in a class system or anything along those lines."

"Good for her!"

"Yes, but not everyone is like her, McMurray."

"Yeah, humans can be a real trip."

"I'm not talking about humans, McMurray. I'm talking about the other dogs."

McMurray stopped eating just short of polishing off the last piece of meat. He stared at Fifi, not really wanting her to continue, but knowing she had to for both their sakes.

"The power we have…"

"When you say "we" you mean the penthouse pooches?"

"Yes. The power we have…the privileges…not all the dogs are as open minded about sharing the wealth."

"What about Bobo and his libertarian upbringing, whatever that is?"

"His humans are libertarian. Bobo is one of the worst of them – of us," she said, looking down in what McMurray interpreted to be shame. "That's why all the dogs got so concerned about what I might have told you about our relationship with humans. You can't let them know I told you that they bow at our paws."

"Why? From what I can see, it's the truth."

"It's supposed to be a secret."

"A secret from who? Us regular mutts?"

Fifi's silence confirmed what McMurray had long suspected

about the order of things. He wondered if his mother, when she warned him and his brothers to stay away from the East Side, knew of what she spoke, or was just repeating something she had been told, something meant to keep her away.

"So, what are you telling me for?"

"Because McMurray – it's wrong. It's wrong that we should have all the power. And there's something special about you. I can tell," Fifi said, averting her gaze from his.

"I have managed to do pretty well for myself, considering."

"That's the other thing I wanted to talk to you about. It's the reason I wanted you to meet me by the park that day. I think I can help you find out what happened to your family."

McMurray paused in the middle of chewing the final piece of filet. There was a long moment of silence between him and Fifi; when he did finally swallow the meat, he was embarrassed by the loud gulping sound it made going down. Even though his mouth was no longer full, he was unable to speak.

"I know it sounds incredible," Fifi said. "But Edith has connections. She donates a lot of money to animal shelters. She can call in favors, you see."

"And why would she do this for me?" McMurray was surprised to hear that his bark with thin and high, warbling as if he might cry. After all these years, the thought of seeing his mother and siblings again was overwhelming.

"Like I said – Edith is a good human. Besides, she wouldn't exactly be doing it for you. She'd be doing it for me. She can see how much I like you." This time, Fifi kept her eyes fixed on McMurray's.

"I… I don't think I'd ever be able to repay you, but I'd be so grateful."

"I don't want anything in return, McMurray, although I welcome your friendship. I'm not just doing this to help you. It's for a larger cause. You see, all of us in this building know what became of our parents and siblings."

"You do? I mean, I know your brother lives next door. But you know where your parents are?" McMurray was shocked.

"Of course. We all have our papers detailing our lineage. My father is Bruno Bowser Leopold and he resides just north of here in the County of Westchester. My mother is Lady Felicia of Marigold. She lives on an estate in Connecticut."

"Wow. You got some pedigree."

"That doesn't mean I'm any more entitled to know what became of my family than you are."

"I get it," McMurray said. "You're looking to shake things up a little. Put the Bobos of the world in their place. And you're looking to use me to do it."

"I'm not using you, McMurray. I just…"

"It's okay, Fi. Can I call you Fi?"

"Of course you may."

"I get how things work. I scratch your belly, you scratch mine."

"Well, I wouldn't put it exactly like that. But I think if we team up, we can do a lot of good together."

"Well, then this is your lucky day, Fi. Because it just so happens that I'm in need of a new partner. But how are you going to get Edith to play along?"

"She already is," Fifi said slyly.

"How so?"

"You're here, aren't you? The logical next step is for her to find out if you have a home."

"She isn't just gonna turn me into the shelter?" McMurray asked, still not trusting Fifi's self-assuredness.

"Of course not. She has too much heart to do something like that."

"She doesn't have too much heart to wear that fancy fur of hers."

"Listen, McMurray. It's not just Bobo and his friends who are snobs. In order for this partnership to work, you're going to have to be a lot less judgmental."

McMurray was taken aback by Fifi's harsh tone. He didn't expect her to be so protective of Mrs. VanCandor. *I really don't know what it's like to have that kind of relationship with a human,* he thought. He wanted to get in Fifi's good graces again as quickly as possible.

"You're right, Fi. Edith's been real good to me so far. I guess, in order for us all to get along, the way you want it, I have to try to be more understanding."

"You're going to have to do more than try, McMurray."

Just then, Mrs. VanCandor came into the kitchen, with Lars following close at her heels, carrying their empty dinner plates.

"Well, my darlings, did you enjoy your supper?" Fifi and McMurray barked and wagged their tails enthusiastically.

"And I see you've cleaned your plates. Very good, my darlings. Here's a cookie for each of you," she continued, reaching into the cabinet and pulling out not a dog biscuit, as McMurray had feared, but something covered in white powder, like snow.

"It's a Linzer torte cookie," Fifi explained. "There's raspberry jam in the middle. It's my absolute favorite!"

"Now, Red, just be careful not to get this powdered sugar all over your nice, clean coat. You really are such a handsome chap, now that you're all cleaned up. Don't you think he's handsome, Lars?"

"Yes, madam," the faithful butler answered.

"I wonder if he belongs to anyone. Is there someone missing you, Red? A little girl crying herself to sleep because her best doggie ran away?" Mrs. VanCandor bent down and held McMurray's face very close to hers when she asked him this. Her blue eyes stared directly into his brown ones; her brow was scrunched as if she was thinking very hard, studying him.

Not a little girl, McMurray thought. *But I wonder if my mother still thinks about me.*

"Well, we're going to have to find out, now aren't we?"

Mrs. VanCandor responded, as if reading his mind. "First thing in the morning I'll have Lila contact all of the animal shelters in the city and see if anyone is looking for a dog that matches your description."

McMurray shot Fifi a confused look. "Edith's personal assistant," she barked.

"I'm glad you agree, Fifi," Mrs. VanCandor said, giving the poodle a loving pat on the head. "Lars, take a picture of Red, won't you? With that pesky cellular phone that I can't seem to figure out how to work? And send it over to Lila with a note that I'll explain tomorrow."

"Yes, madam."

"Now, my darlings, I must catch up on my correspondence before turning in. Lars, thank you for another wonderful meal. I'll see you in the morning."

Lars bowed slightly at the waist as Mrs. VanCandor left the room. Following her orders, he promptly took a photo of McMurray, who had just finished licking the last of the powdered sugar from his lips.

"That will do," Lars said, as he snapped the phone shut. "Now, let's take our evening constitutional, shall we?"

"Our what?" McMurray asked Fifi.

"It means walk."

"Well, why can't he just say walk? It takes a lot less time than spitting out the word constitutional."

"Did you not just agree ten minutes ago to be less judgmental, McMurray?"

"Well, I can tell from all this yapping that you two are eager for some fresh air," Lars interrupted. "Let's get on with it."

"Sorry, Fi," McMurray groaned quietly as they headed toward the elevator. His apology received no response.

The three of them – Lars, McMurray and Fifi – walked in silence. It was a chilly evening, and when McMurray got back inside he was grateful for the warmth of the heated linoleum in the laundry room, where he slept soundly the whole night through. He wasn't sure where Fifi had retired to; she hadn't even wished him a good night. As he drifted off to sleep, he told himself that he'd make it up to her in the morning. In his last moments of consciousness, he was also able to admit to himself that despite his first impression of Edith VanCandor, she was turning out to be a very good hostess.

CHAPTER EIGHT –

A Walk Down Memory Lane

THE NEXT MORNING, MCMURRAY woke to the smell of scrambled eggs and bacon. After stretching his limbs, he sauntered into the kitchen where he found Fifi finishing up her breakfast and Lars sipping coffee out of a very large mug. McMurray was familiar with the ritual of breakfast from his time with the Farbers; Mr. Farber, in response to his son's insatiable curiosity, always said he couldn't answer any questions until after he'd had his morning coffee. And like Mr. Farber did every day, Lars was thumbing through a newspaper, which he put aside to serve McMurray.

"Where's Edith?" McMurray asked Fifi while Lars prepared his plate.

"I'm going as fast as I can. It's not my fault you overslept and now your breakfast is cold," Lars said, misunderstanding.

"She's doing what she said she'd do. She's meeting with Lila about you. And good morning, by the way," Fifi said.

"Oh, I see. You two are having a morning chat," Lars noted, back in the swing of things again.

"Good morning, Fi. Look, I'm going to try to be better

today. Every day. From here on in, I'm gonna be the most lovable mutt you ever knew."

To prove it, after breakfast when they were out walking with Wyatt and the other dogs, McMurray went out of his way to be friendly. "So, Bobo. How's that bum hip feeling? It looks like you've got a little more spring in your step today."

"I dare say it feels a little better. Thank you for asking chap. I don't have to ask why you're in such a good mood this morning, what with your makeover giving you a glow on the outside and the bounty of Mrs. VanCandor's table warming your insides."

McMurray thought he sensed some unfriendliness in Bobo's tone, but decided to ignore it. "Yes, Edith – I mean Mrs. VanCandor – has been very generous, very kind. I'm very fortunate that she took me in."

"It's not so much that she took you in, but that you foisted yourself upon her," Fernando interjected. "What's the correct term? Crashed? Yes, that's it. You crashed our group."

"It's true that I tagged along yesterday, but Mrs. VanCandor didn't have to welcome me into her home. I didn't expect that," McMurray said in his defense.

"No, you couldn't possibly have. But our friend, Fifi, here – that's a different story," Bobo said snidely. "Fifi, tell us. How did you meet Red prior to him crashing our walk yesterday?"

"I thought you gathered from your eavesdropping yesterday, Bobo – we met when Wyatt was still walking just me, right outside Central Park. Running into each other yesterday was just a happy coincidence."

"It seems strange that a dog like Red would wander into a neighborhood like this, and happen upon a charming canine such as yourself, Fi, purely by coincidence."

"Like I told you yesterday, Bobo – it's a free country," McMurray said, sounding more uptight than he'd intended.

"All right. No need to get excited, Red, my boy," Bobo

responded condescendingly. "Just relax and take in the sights…
enjoy this little vacation while it lasts."

"The name's McMurray."

"What?" the dogs all asked at once.

"My name – it's McMurray. Not Red. It's McMurray."

"Well, no need to get testy. How were we supposed
to know?" Fernando said. "You'd better watch your tone,
McMurray. No one likes a vicious dog, especially one that
probably hasn't had his shots."

"Fernando, be nice!" Fifi demanded.

"Oh, Fi. You're always trying to make the world a better
place."

"And what's wrong with that, Nando?"

"Nothing, dear sister. Except some of us like the world the
way it is."

Wyatt removed his headphones and pulled on the leashes.
McMurray knew he'd never get used to the sensation of the
choke collar tightening around his neck. "What's all this
barking going on here? I can't hear my Rachmaninoff."

The dogs just stared up at him innocently. The Epstein
twins, who McMurray noted tended to keep to themselves,
barked, "It wasn't us!"

"All right. Well, just settle down, okay?"

For the rest of the walk, the dogs didn't speak, but the
knowing glances Bobo and Fernando exchanged didn't
escape McMurray's notice. When he and Fifi got back to
Mrs. VanCandor's and were safely out of earshot of everyone,
including Lars who had gone to the market, McMurray sat Fifi
down for a serious talk.

"Bobo and your brother think you're up to something,
Fi."

"They think. They suspect it. They don't know."

"Yeah, well it didn't take long for them to suspect it. Have
you pulled something like this before?"

"Never, I swear! I used to talk to them – mostly Nando –

about sharing our power with others less fortunate, but when I realized what I was up against, I stopped and decided to take matters into my own paws. Still, they know what my feelings are."

"*Others less fortunate?* I'm not a charity case, Fifi."

"I know you're not. Of course you're not. Look, the others will come around. Kill them with kindness, as the saying goes."

"I was very nice today, Fi, and they wanted no part of it."

"They're just used to being the alpha dogs, that's all. They need some time to adjust to there being a new member of the pack."

"If they ran into Malachi, he could maybe help them with that."

"Whose Malachi?"

"Malachi leads a pack in Central Park. They're real tough guys."

"Tougher than you?" Fifi asked sheepishly.

"Much tougher than me," McMurray said. "Those canines got no scruples."

"Well, let's hope it doesn't come to that. Edith will be home soon. Maybe she'll have some good news."

"I don't see how she could track down my family, with nothing to go on. It's been years since I was at the shelter, since we were separated."

"Well, then – perhaps you'll have to give her something to go on. If Edith can't find out anything on her own, perhaps tomorrow during our walk we should take a detour over to the West Side, to the house you lived in with your family. Wyatt has proved very helpful thus far."

McMurray chuckled to himself at the way Fifi talked: *thus far.* But he knew better than to make fun of her, or any of her friends, out loud again. Also, her plan wasn't a bad one. If he could communicate to Wyatt where he was born, and Wyatt could communicate it to Edith, then just maybe there was a chance. For as he suspected, when Mrs. VanCandor arrived home, she did so bearing no good news; there was no trace of McMurray in the system, and no one recognized his photo.

"Don't give up hope, my darlings. Lila is going to put posters up all around the neighborhood and the park. Until we figure something out, you can stay here with us, Red." Then Mrs. VanCandor kissed McMurray on the nose.

There was no way for him to tell her what his real name was, and when she came near him the musky scent of her perfume made him so dizzy he could barely remember it himself. He was grateful for all she was doing for him, and to show it, he gave her a slobbery kiss on the cheek, which caused her to giggle wildly.

"You are a rascal, aren't you?" she asked him.

"Darn right!" he barked back, winking at Fi.

That night they dined on duck and then went for their evening constitutional. Fifi turned in shortly afterward; McMurray discovered she had her own room adjacent to Mrs. VanCandor's. It seemed the cat, Macy, was too territorial to allow anyone else in to Mrs. VanCandor's bedroom. McMurray slept in the laundry room again. Lars had put a load of wash in the dryer before retiring to his quarters, and the sound of the machine's motor and the clothes turning over and over helped put McMurray's mind, which was now working overtime, to rest.

The next morning when Wyatt came to pick them up, McMurray and Fifi carried out their plan. They steered Wyatt – who was as easily steered as ever – through the park, over to the West Side. As fortune would have it, Bobo had a veterinary appointment that morning, so it was only Fernando's complaints they had to deal with. The Epstein twins, as usual, were just happy to be along for the walk.

"Exactly why is it we must traipse all the way over to this side of the city, dear sister?"

"Because we never do, Nando, and I'm tired of passing the

same buildings, seeing the same humans. Don't you ever feeling like sniffing a new tree?"

"Yes, I suppose it does a dog good to get out of his comfort zone every now and then and acquaint himself with some new scenery," Fernando conceded. "But this is a rather far distance we're traveling, don't you think?"

"Winter will be here soon and everything will be covered with dirty snow. Let's enjoy the chance to roam while we can, shall we?"

Fifi's common sense arguments silenced Fernando for a while. McMurray realized it was in his best interest not to say much when he was among this group – that is, until they arrived at the Chumpskis' brownstone. Then he started howling at the top of his lungs. Because Fernando couldn't be trusted, McMurray couldn't let it slip that they were standing in front of the home where he was born and lived happily for several months with his mother and brothers. Instead, he just made a tremendous fuss, hoping to signal to Wyatt that this place was significant.

"What are you doin' boy? What's the matter?" Wyatt asked.

"Yes, McMurray – what *are* you doing? You're causing a scene," said Fernando, as he dramatically covered his eyes with one of his paws.

McMurray just kept on yelping and wailing. He even got up on his back feet and twirled around. Finally, Wyatt got the picture. "Does this house mean something to you? Is this your home?"

Wyatt pulled on McMurray's leash to get him to move on, but he would not budge, not even when the collar got so tight around his neck that he did, indeed, start choking. "Well, I guess that's a yes. It's okay boy," Wyatt said, attempting to comfort McMurray with a few pats on the head.

The goodhearted dog walker went up to the Chumpskis' front door and rang the bell, but no one answered. He took a notebook out of his backpack and McMurray watched, elated, as Wyatt wrote down the address. When they got back to Mrs. VanCandor's later, Wyatt didn't disappoint.

"Red got all excited when we passed the house at this address," he said, handing the piece of notebook paper to Mrs. VanCandor. "No one was home, but it seemed this place was real important to Red, so maybe someone should check back."

"Oh, thank you, Wyatt. This seems very promising indeed! Tell me – why did you decide to walk to the West Side today?" Mrs. VanCandor asked.

"That's where the dogs wanted to go," Wyatt responded, scratching his head.

"Maybe Red was trying to make his way back home!"

Mrs. VanCandor clapped her hands together, seeming every bit as excited as McMurray felt. "Thank you!" he barked to everyone in the room.

"I told you!" Fifi answered back.

Mrs. VanCandor immediately got Lila on the phone and asked her to trace the address. McMurray paced back and forth in the library, listening to Mrs. VanCandor's make appointments with her tailor, her manicurist, and her acupuncturist before Lila called back. "What's that dear? The Chumpskis you say? My, what an interesting name. Do you have a number for Mr. Chumpski? No, no – I want to call them myself. Yes, of course. I have a pen and paper right here."

McMurray studied Mrs. VanCandor's hand as she took the number down from Lila. He wasn't sure where it would all lead, but at least it *was* a lead. He sat in front of her, staring pensively. Fifi was curled up in a chair across the room. "Patience is a virtue!" she called over to him.

"I've been patient! Now I want answers. Besides, this was all your idea. Aren't you in the least bit excited to see if you can pull it off?"

"My darlings, please! I'm on the phone!" Mrs. VanCandor reprimanded.

"I know I can!" Fifi barked, getting in the last word between them.

"Hello, is this Mr. Chumpski? Oh, good! This is Edith VanCandor. You don't know me...no, this is not a telemarketing call. I'm phoning to see if you lost a dog recently? Oh, no? Well, have you ever had a dog, or to your knowledge has there ever been a dog living at your address? You see, I found a dog – or rather he found me – and he seems to feel a connection to your property. Really? Oh, do tell! How absolutely charming. Five pups, you say? In your basement? Imagine that! Do you by any chance remember the date? You do! Oh, I see – it was the weekend of your parents' 50th anniversary. And do you recall what shelter they were taken to? Yes, it has been a long time. Yes, I'll check with Animal Control. Thank you for your time, Mr. Chumpski. Good day."

Without missing a beat, Mrs. VanCandor had Lila back on the phone. "Dear, I need a favor from Morris. I need to track down a record of a call Animal Control made to a residence on the Upper West Side about seven years ago. I know, but he'll do it for me, dear. I've donated a lot of money to his wife's favorite charity. If he needs reminding of that, feel free to do so."

Mrs. VanCandor gave Lila the details of the call Animal Control made to the Chumpskis' home all those years ago, to take away a mother dog and her five male pups who had been living quite well in the basement until a pipe burst, flooding them out. It was difficult for McMurray to relive the details, but his anticipation outweighed his sadness. *Maybe I really am going to see my family again,* he thought.

That dream grew closer to becoming a reality when, 45 minutes later, Mrs. VanCandor's friend Morris called with the information she had requested.

CHAPTER NINE –

It's a Dog's Life

"LARS! LARS!" MRS. VANCANDOR SHOUTED as she ran from the library into what she referred to as the parlor. McMurray and Fifi were close behind.

"What is it, madam?"

"Morris…you know Morris?"

"Yes, your friend down at the mayor's office."

"That's the one! Well, Morris is sending over a file that contains all the information about Red's history – as much as they have anyway."

"Wonderful, madam! Congratulations on solving the mystery."

McMurray and Fifi exchanged knowing glances as Lars continued, "So you now know where his home is?"

"Not exactly. Shortly after he was brought to the shelter as a puppy, he was adopted by a family called the Farbers. But the Farbers reported him missing to that same shelter less than a month later. The records don't show that he was ever found."

"So that's where the trail runs cold, so to speak."

"Yes, so to speak, Lars."

"What about my mother? What about my brothers?" demanded McMurray.

Just then, the phone buzzed in a way McMurray had come to recognize as the front desk calling to inform Mrs. VanCandor of one thing or another. "That can't be the file already!" she exclaimed, as Lars picked up the receiver.

"Who did you say it was? Eddie? We don't know any Eddie. Madam, do we know a gentleman named Eddie?" Lars asked, cupping his hand over the mouthpiece.

"No, I don't think so. Does he have a file with him, Lars?"

"Does he have a file? Really? Interesting. Madam, he has one of the posters Lila put up, with Red's photo on it. He says Red is his dog."

McMurray and Fifi looked at each other, wide eyed. In the face of this unexpected turn of events, McMurray found that he had momentarily lost the ability to bark.

"Shall I have him sent up, madam?"

"Well…yes, I suppose so. Thank you, Lars."

Not three minutes later, the elevator door slid open, and out stepped Eddie, looking much more dapper than the last time McMurray laid eyes on him. His formerly unruly facial hair was carefully trimmed, as was the hair on his head. The suit and shoes he was wearing looked new, as did the hat he politely removed from the top of his head upon entering Fifi and Mrs. VanCandor's home. It was the first time McMurray had seen him without his guitar.

"Good day, ma'am. My, my…that dog sure has done well for himself. This is a swell place you got here."

"Why thank you, sir. I'm sorry, I didn't catch your last name," Mrs. VanCandor said, extending her hand.

"No need for such formalities. You can just call me Eddie. Everybody does."

"All right, Eddie. I'm Edith. This is Lars, my butler and good friend. And this is Fifi, my best friend. And I guess you know who this is," she said, motioning to McMurray. "Although I must say, he doesn't look all that excited to see you. Are you sure he's your dog?"

"Well, I suppose he's my dog as much as he can be anybody's dog. He's more my partner. We had a gig going outside the Metropolitan Museum. But then I got sick, you see. They called my daughter and she came up and tended to me. Set me up with some new threads. I was all ready to get back to performin', but it seems I lost my partner. Then I saw your poster and, well, I thought I'd come by and see if he wanted to strike things up again. Looks like he got it pretty good here though."

"So, this dog, he's not really yours? He's a stray?" Mrs. VanCandor asked. "Does he have a name?"

"I don't know if he's got a name. I just call him dog."

Touched by Eddie's loyalty, McMurray went over and jumped on him, in the best display of a hug he could manage. "Well, it's good to see you too, dog," Eddie said, rubbing him behind his ears.

Then the phone buzzed again. This time, it was the messenger Morris sent over with the file; Lars ran down to get it, and while he was gone, Eddie and Mrs. VanCandor made polite conversation. "So, you're a musician?" she asked him. "What kind of music do you play?"

"Blues guitar, ma'am. Yup, I sing some pretty mean blues. I used to perform in all the hot clubs, but you know...let's just say I had a spat of bad luck. By the time I got my act together, well – it's hard to start over when you're an old man."

"Nonsense, Eddie! I'd love to hear you play some time. I'm a generous patron of the arts."

Just then, Lars came in waving the file. "I got it!" he shouted triumphantly. McMurray and Fifi ran over to him, jumping up and down. "Settle down, now. The last time I checked, dogs couldn't read," he said, handing the file to Mrs. VanCandor.

McMurray looked at Fifi questioningly. "It's true," Fifi barked. "We may be highly cultured, but we still have our limitations."

"Well, Morris did an excellent job. All of the information is right here. The mother, she was about four or five at the time, by the shelter's estimate, was adopted by a family in Cobble Hill. Two of the boys went together to a family in TriBeCa – much more residential there now than it used to be. One pup went to Queens, and the remaining boy went to Staten Island. My goodness, this family got spread out all over the city! And Red here – oh, my, that's funny. The shelter named him Erik the Red. What a coincidence."

"My coat is red! It's not that big of a leap!" McMurray barked, wishing Mrs. VanCandor would stick to the relevant points.

"He lived with a family in Brooklyn Heights for just a very short while. He fled from the back of the car when they were stopped at a gas station, according to the report. I wonder if he's been on his own ever since," Mrs. VanCandor pondered.

"You bet I have!"

"I'd bet so," Eddie spoke on McMurray's behalf. "He's a very independent minded pooch. Question is, does he want to continue on that way?"

"Yes, McMurray – that is the question," Fifi joined in. "Are you going to go with Eddie, or stay here with us?"

"I haven't gotten an invitation to stay," McMurray said.

"Shhh! My darlings, stop all this noise," Mrs. VanCandor interrupted. "Now, Eddie, you have no proof that this dog is yours, and I don't believe in dogs living on the street, but if he wants to go with you, I'm not going to put my foot down about it. If he doesn't, well, he can stay here with us."

"There's your invitation!"

"Fifi, quiet, please!" Mrs. VanCandor reprimanded.

McMurray watched as Eddie studied all of Mrs. VanCandor's fine things. Eddie would want what was best for him, he knew that. *But what do I want?* McMurray asked himself. He did have a nice set-up with Mrs. VanCandor. And then there was Fifi. He looked over at her; as soon as their eyes met, she looked away. *Sweet, Fifi,* he thought. *Could this be more than friendship?* Then his mind turned to his mother and brothers. He'd just found out where they were. *What will give me the best chance of seeing them again?* he wondered. *And how much of this is actually in my paws?*

As if to answer his last question, Eddie stepped in. "Far be it for me to decide how anyone should live his life, but I do have an idea that might be in everyone's best interest – including mine."

"Go ahead, Eddie," Mrs. VanCandor encouraged. "What's your idea?"

"Well, ma'am, since you said you're a patron of the arts, I was wondering if maybe you'd help support them by letting this here dog continue working with me. I could come by and pick him up each morning, and we could go to the museum. Then I'd bring him back here each night. This way, I still have my partner, and this dog has a nice place to rest his head at night."

"And what about you, Eddie? Do you have a nice place to rest your head at night?"

"Oh, yes ma'am. I have one of those efficiency units in Queens. It's not much, but it's enough. Can't have dogs there though."

McMurray's ears perked up at the mention of Queens. *That's where one of my brothers is. Maybe Eddie could help,* he thought. He liked the sound of Eddie's idea on other counts as well; it allowed him to maintain some of his freedom, and it meant he'd still get to see Fifi on a regular basis.

"Well, my darlings, what do you think?"

Both McMurray and Fifi sounded their approval of the plan with enthusiastic barks, to which Mrs. VanCandor responded, "That settles it, then! Red...Dog...we'll have to figure that out later…but he'll work with you during the day, Eddie, and spend his evenings with us. He gets weekends off though," she clarified, wagging a finger at Eddie. "And of course you're also welcome here any time," she said warmly.

Lars rolled his eyes at Mrs. VanCandor's open invitation to Eddie. "Another stray," McMurray heard him mutter under his breath, but in keeping with his promise to Fifi, he tried not to judge Lars too poorly for it.

"We'll have to take him to the vet and get him properly licensed of course, to keep Animal Control at bay. What's in this file should suffice as evidence that the dog we've been calling Red – the dog you refer to as Dog – currently has no rightful owner. I'll put it in the library for safe keeping," Mrs. VanCandor explained. "Now that that's settled, would you like to stay for dinner, Eddie?"

"No, thank you ma'am. My daughter enrolled me in one of those fitness classes at the Y and I don't want to be late. I promised her, you know. But I am much obliged," Eddie said as he tipped as hat to her before placing it on his head. "Dog, I'll see you bright and early tomorrow. It's only been a couple of weeks, but I sure hope you haven't gotten rusty," he warned.

"No, sir!" McMurray barked back.

"Nice to have you back, partner!" Eddie said as he disappeared into the elevator.

"Speaking of dinner, I'm famished, Lars. What will it be tonight, my darlings? How about some venison stew?"

"Yes, madam," Lars said as he retreated into the kitchen.

McMurray and Fifi followed Mrs. VanCandor into the library, where they watched her place the folder containing the information about McMurray's family in her desk drawer. The next question to be answered was whether or not it was going to stay there.

CHAPTER TEN –

Moving Up and Moving On

McMurray and Fifi didn't say much to each other that evening. In the morning, Eddie was there bright and early, as promised, which saved McMurray from having to face the gang of penthouse pooches during their daily group walk. McMurray did have time to eat some breakfast before he left; he was pleased to hear Lars offer Eddie some coffee and eggs without being prompted to by Mrs. VanCandor.

Mrs. VanCandor told Eddie he should keep McMurray on a leash when they were walking on the street together, and Eddie politely obeyed; but to McMurray's relief, Eddie took the leash off as soon as they cleared the first corner. All the way to the museum, McMurray got to walk freely – his own dog, once more. And he proved to Eddie that he wasn't at all rusty. All day long, he jumped higher and twirled faster than he ever had before. He worked the crowd, whenever there was one, by offering children his paw, rolling over, and playing dead. It was okay to do these things, he reconciled, because he wasn't being asked to, he was choosing to.

"The two of us almost look too good now to be street performers," Eddie mentioned to him when he was counting the day's take. "It didn't hurt us any. This is a pretty good haul."

On the way to the penthouse that evening, they stopped for dinner the way they usually did. "Now dog, I can't eat that greasy food anymore. I promised my daughter. We didn't talk for a long time before I got sick and I'm not gonna go breaking any promises I made to her. But if you still want your moo shu, I'll get it for you. Me, I'm getting a veggie burger from that health food place across the street."

McMurray stood in front of the Chinese restaurant and barked, twirling around on his haunches. "Moo shu it is!" Eddie said. "Oh, it must be good to be young." He returned less than ten minutes later with the food. *As good as the eats are at Fifi's house, nothing tastes as good as when you earn it yourself,* McMurray thought. All in all, it had been a good day; unfortunately, it didn't stay that way.

"The penthouse pooches are furious," Fifi told him when he saw her later that evening.

"About what?"

"About you, McMurray. They know that you'll be staying here permanently. They know about the file."

"And just how do they know all that?" McMurray barked at her, sounding meaner than he meant to.

"Edith told Fernando's human and he overheard, then Fernando told the rest of the group. The whole block knows. They're calling me a traitor. They want you out of here."

"I'm not going anywhere without that file!"

Fifi put her head down. "Is that all you care about, McMurray? The file? I thought you might find it a little difficult to leave me."

"Of course I'd miss you, Fi. But I'm so close to seeing my family again. I can't give up now. Who knows what conditions they might be living in? My mother isn't young anymore. I have to try to see her at least one more time."

"I'm sorry, McMurray. I know I started this. But you

weren't there today. Bobo and Fernando were so vicious. Wyatt actually had to muzzle Nando. I expected to be reproached by Bobo, but to be threatened by my own brother..."

"Do you want me to go with you tomorrow, to protect you?"

"Goodness no, McMurray! That would only make things worse. You need to avoid the group for now, give them time to calm down. I'm sure they will, once they see that there's no reason to distrust you. But that means you can't tell other dogs about that file."

"Why? What's in that file is no skin off the noses of the penthouse pooches. It's got nothing to do with them."

"It's not what's in the file. It's that I got you the file – that I showed you how to get it. If all of the canines in the city knew the power we wielded, they'd want it too, and there's a chance that we'd be dethroned – that we wouldn't be top dogs anymore. "

"I thought that's what you wanted. A city of equals."

"It is…but primarily I want to help you."

"Well, help me then. Help me figure out how to use the information in that file to find my family."

"For you McMurray, I'd do almost anything. But it may have to be enough that you know where your mother and brothers are. Do you think you can live with that? After all, it's been a long time since you all left the shelter. They may not even be at those addresses anymore. Are you willing to risk everything for an unknown? Are you willing to risk me?"

She must really be scared, McMurray thought to himself, *to be changing her tune like this. Or maybe she's just being a woman – Eddie always said they like to change their minds.* Before McMurray could figure out what his answer to Fi's question was, Lars came in to take them for their constitutional. "To be continued," McMurray barked.

After the walk, the three of them – Lars, Fifi and McMurray – were waiting for the elevator to take them back up to the penthouse. When the door slid open, McMurray was surprised to see Fernando inside with a human; he'd only ever seen him on their group walks. *This encounter seems too perfect to be happening by chance,* McMurray thought.

"Good evening, Mrs. Casablanca," Lars said politely to the human.

"Good evening, Lars. Wonderful night for a brisk walk."

"Quite right, Mrs. Casablanca."

As the two were exchanging pleasantries, Fernando was growling under his breath: "A smart dog knows when to leave well enough alone." And then he was gone out the front door with Mrs. Casablanca.

That night, McMurray tossed and turned on his newly bought bed – an official welcome present from Mrs. VanCandor. The bed was quite comfortable, and McMurray found the sounds of the dryer as soothing as ever. It wasn't even Fifi's near admission of love that was keeping him awake; it was what Fernando said, about leaving well enough alone. *I do have it pretty good here. The best roof over my head that money can buy. Generous humans. An honest business partner. And then there's Fi… She was trying to make the same point Fernando was, about being content. It's not hard to be content with Fi…*

When McMurray finally did drift off, he was thinking about her, and the happy future they might be able to have together, if only he could forget about his past.

As the weeks passed, and winter took hold of the city with full force, that appeared to be what happened. McMurray, content to be living life on his own terms, thought about the file in the library less and less. He developed a cordial, albeit distanced, relationship with the penthouse pooches. And he developed a more than cordial relationship with Fi.

He and Eddie didn't perform when the weather was too brutal, so that snowy winter McMurray ended up spending a lot of time indoors, in front of the fireplace in the parlor, with Fi and Mrs. VanCandor. Eddie took Mrs. VanCandor up on her invitation and stopped by from time to time. Lars was thrilled to learn that Eddie was a formidable chess player, and the two of them ended up getting along quite famously. By the time the first signs of spring had sprung, the five of them had become a somewhat unusual, but rather happy, family. And when it came down to it, family was what McMurray had been after.

There were times, when McMurray saw a stray dog in the park, that he felt a twinge of guilt over his good fortune. He comforted himself by focusing on the fact that although he lived on the Upper East Side, he was a working dog, not like the penthouse pooches in his building. He was glad they still looked at him as an outsider. For our hero, McMurray, had made a pact with himself: *If ever he was to truly forget where he came from, if ever forgot his roots, he would get to that file in the library and find them, regardless of what it meant to the balance of power.* For that is what heroes do.

Until that day, if it came, there was no doubt that McMurray, Fifi, Mrs. VanCandor, Lars and Eddie – and even Macy and Topaz – would all live happily ever after.